June Caravel

The curse of holiday romance

Novel

FROM THE SAME AUTHOR...

Other books from the same author are about to come out or have already been released...

To discover the entire universe of June Caravel, go to http://www.junecaravel.com.

You will receive free excerpts and know before everybody when the next books will be released by subscribing to the newsletter.

Already released:

— The curse of holiday romance, 2020

— Pregnant at any price!, Creo Éditions, 2021

To be released:

— Wild Card, 2022

© June Caravel 2021
www.junecaravel.com

Illustration: Félix Rousseau

Édition : BoD – Books on Demand, 12/14 rond-point des Champs-Élysées, 75008 Paris
Impression : BoD - Books on Demand, Norderstedt, Allemagne

ISBN : 978-2-322155-67-5
Registration of copyright: November 2021

All rights reserved for all countries

CHAPTER ONE
THE CURSE

Miguel tried to kiss me in front of everyone. I was livid. I had turned him down, several times already during my holiday, so why did he keep on trying? I slapped him instinctively.

"Are you crazy or something?"

Incredulous, Miguel started massaging his left cheek. Everybody was silent and looked at me dumbfounded. No one expected such a violent reaction from me.

Then his cousins sitting around the table had all burst into laughter. Miguel glared sternly at them and those who were still laughing stopped instantly. He stood up and closed his eyes, concentrating on who knows what. All of a sudden, Miguel's body started trembling from head to toe. It was as if he was in trance. I thought he was having an epileptic fit. When he opened his eyes, it was as if he was possessed. He held both his arms in my direction and said:

"You can forget about having a holiday romance! If you ever come close to having one in the future, this will ensure that disaster will strike!"

It was as if a supernatural voice had taken over him. My body was shaking. I couldn't help it. He tightened his right hand as if he was going to strangle me remotely. I couldn't breathe anymore. Then he lowered his arm and fled into his room. The trembling, the sensation of choking went away at once. I took a deep breath. I couldn't explain what had just happened. It was as if he had cast a spell on me.

Luana, my best friend, took me by the arm into the living room, where the rest of the family was singing and dancing.

"Don't worry about it..." she said. "My cousin Miguel's father is a shaman so he thinks he's got powers too and that he can cast spells."

"Hold on, can you repeat that? Your uncle is a shaman?"

"Yes, shamans are aplenty in Mexico…"

I didn't know what a shaman was, but from her tone, I deduced it was some sort of magician.

"But what does a shaman do, exactly?" I asked.

"A shaman cures souls and sicknesses. Look, don't take these threats too seriously. He's been crazy about you ever since he saw you arrive. He is just trying to scare you because you refused his advances, but really, he's harmless."

"But you saw it with your own eyes earlier... The transformation in his face. It was as if he was... possessed…"

"Don't worry. You slapped him in front of his cousins and he probably just wanted to scare you. I think it's the first time a girl has turned him down."

Luana took me by the hand and we started dancing. Miguel didn't reappear the whole night. The next day we left at dawn to avoid traffic. I never saw him again.

CHAPTER 2
HOLIDAYS IN MEXICO

Since this incident, I had to admit, that every time I went on holidays with my parents, Luana or other friends, and that I was single, almost everyone found a holiday romance except for me. I had started to call it «The curse of holiday romance».

Despite my efforts–and believe me, I tried everything– sexy dresses, squeezing guys tight while dancing, talking endlessly until the small hours–. Something always happened the moment I was about to finally kiss the guy. Once I had a tummy bug, which flared up the moment I was one inch away from kissing the guy I had been chasing the whole week. He had ended up with someone from another class.

While on holiday with friends in Malta, I suddenly had nausea and threw up the entire meal I had just eaten over the guy I fancied. He ran away to have a shower. Understandably he avoided me until the end of our stay. He even went as far as to make fun of me by mimicking me vomiting whenever he saw me.

Another time, on holidays with Luana when we were students, I had gone for a swim with Matthew, a friend of Luana who lived in the Sables d'Olonne and who I was attracted to since the beginning of our vacation. He had taken me in his arms and we were about to kiss, when a jellyfish stung me. I have no idea how it managed to leave him unscathed since we were entwined. I was in such pain I had to get out of the water and ask the lifeguards for help. Matthew had accompanied me but had soon said he had something to do and disappeared. We didn't have cell phones back then but strangely we never crossed paths despite having bumped into each other every day before the incident. I had finally discovered he had found someone else in the meantime.

So when I accepted Luana's invitation to go to Mexico, her homeland, the year of my 28th birthday for a three weeks trip, I really hoped that the curse would finally stop. Maybe it was the fact that I was going to Mexico, Miguel's homeland, which made me hope that I would close the loop. Surely this curse would stop on shamanic land? It was ridiculous: it had lasted 14 years!

Every time I had gone on holidays with Luana, I reminded her of the episode with Miguel and she dismissed it. She was convinced it was nothing. That Miguel had no power whatsoever. But when I asked if we were going to see her cousin in Mexico, she said she didn't know if he would be there.

Luana had flown several times to Mexico all these years and she had seen her cousin Miguel again. She had told me he had become a shaman like his father and that she had accidentally witnessed a shamanic ceremony where her cousin was in charge.

She arrived at his place as he was curing a young woman lying on a mat on the ground. He was now married and his wife who was drumming on a tambourine gestured Luana to sit down and shut up. The girl seemed possessed, she was trembling all over. Miguel did as if he was absorbing the disease through his mouth in several parts of his patient's body. Then he had spit it away in a bowl and thrown away the content outside of the window. During the whole ceremony, Miguel hadn't seem to realize even one second that Luana was there. It's only when the girl had opened her eyes and that the drumming stopped that he had smiled to her, gesturing her to wait until he was finished with the young girl.

This tale had chilled me to my bones. No matter how cartesian I was, this curse that was baiting on me was all supernatural. I had to understand its mechanism. Most of all, I hoped what happened was now water under the bridge. Maybe I could have asked Miguel to cancel the curse. Luana never stopped telling me that maybe my subconscious had turned it into a self-fulfilling prophecy. I thought she was exaggerating. I never wanted to have a tummy bug, or retch as I was about to kiss a guy! And how about the jellyfish case? I couldn't explain why it only stung me and not Matthew or why it was even in the Atlantic ocean, which was not exactly as well-known as Mediterranean for the presence of jellyfish.

During our stay, we went to see Luana's family that I had not seen since the fateful holiday when I was 14. They told me Miguel now lived a hundred miles away from where we were staying. The fact that he had become a shaman reinforced my feeling that this curse was very real and that Luana's cousin had much more power than she would admit. I asked my best friend if we could go and see him. Luana's cousins weren't too happy with my suggestion.

"I don't think it's a good idea, Julia." said one of them.

"Why?" I asked.

"He's still mad at you for slapping him. I'm not sure he would be happy to see you."

"What if I went to apologize? It's 14 years ago, for goodness sake!"

I knelt down in front of Luana. I needed to see Miguel to understand what had really happened. If he had really cast a spell on me, I wanted to know if he could reverse it. Luana picked up the phone.

"What's his number?" she asked. "I'm going to call him."

Her grandmother stood up and dialed the number for her. I didn't understand the whole conversation that followed since my Spanish was not very good. Luana hung up.

"We're going tomorrow."

"You said I was going to be there?"

"Yes."

"Is he still mad at me?"

"I don't know. I don't think so. He said we were both welcome."

I had a nightmare that night. I saw an arm slowly stretching out towards me while I was running away to escape. I turned around my head as I ran to see whose arm it was, but I could only see it getting closer and closer… until it caught my neck and tightened its grip. I couldn't breathe. The hand carried on tightening and…I woke up all of a sudden trying to catch my breath. The sensation was still there, as if it had really happened. It did not bode well. I wasn't so sure I wanted to see Miguel again.

I didn't manage to get back to sleep that night. I arrived very tired at his house and a little bit anxious at the idea of seeing the man whose curse had been plaguing me all these years…

A woman carrying a baby and a little boy of about three years old welcomed us. She couldn't speak French. Luana told me she was Miguel's wife. Now that he was married, at least he would not try to hit on me this time!

His wife was very nice to me. She asked if I wanted something to drink. Luana started talking in Spanish and she translated that Miguel wouldn't be long. The children were adorable until his wife put the cute little baby in my arms. It started to scream as soon as I held it and I had to give it back to her mum straight away. At last Miguel arrived.

I almost didn't recognize him. He wore a traditional Mexican shirt. He had simply become a man, and a cute one at that. I almost regretted not having gone out with him when I was younger. He welcomed us with a large smile, which warmed my heart given the circumstances of our last encounter. He hugged Luana and then held me in his arms.

"Hello Julia, I thought I would never see you again."

"Neither, did I. I came to apologize."

He gave me a charming smile.

"It's an old story. Don't worry. I had forgotten about it."

"Are you sure?"

"Yes, of course."

"Then why am I still cursed?"

He stared at me astonished. I continued:

"Ever since you said those words, I have never had a holiday romance. Every time I go on holiday, there's always something that stops me from kissing guys at the last minute."

Luana cut me short:

"I've been telling her to stop believing in this curse for years, but she won't let it go. Did you really cast a spell on her, Miguel?"

Miguel looked at his feet and mumbled:

"Let's just say that... I didn't think it would work."

Luana stared at Miguel incredulous:

"What do you mean?" she asked.

Miguel seemed a bit uneasy.

"My father told me never to use the power of the spirits to take revenge. I have never done it since. It served me as a lesson."

"You mean that all these years...?"

I gasped for air. I sat down. Luana carried on:

"I always thought it was nonsense. How is it possible? You're a true wizard then?"

"No, it's not exactly how it works. I have no powers. I'm just a channel. The spirits do the work."

"So then it means you can stop the curse, can't you?" I asked.

Miguel looked at me with a sorry look.

"Unfortunately, no. I can't undo what has been said. And believe me Julia, I've been feeling guilty about it these past fourteen years. On that night I felt rejected, humiliated and upset. I don't know why I put that curse on you. It was beyond my control. I didn't think."

"But why can't you undo the curse?"

"Because if I undo it, who knows what will happen? It could be worse. The spirits are cunning and want something else in exchange of what they gave. Believe me it's better to leave things this way. And then, it's not so bad, is it? You can fall in love with someone outside of holiday, can't you?"

"Let's say it's a pain when someone I'm attracted to on holiday ends up in the arms of someone else. And the worst thing is that whatever I do, whenever I decide to go on holiday somewhere and I have a boyfriend, my relationships always end just before I go. Sometimes even at the last minute. So I'm condemned to never go on holidays again or to brave the curse. But you also said there would be a great disaster if I tried to have a holiday romance, didn't you?"

"I did say that, yes."

"What kind?"

"Only the spirits know. It could be anything: a storm, a tsunami, a fire, an accident. I wasn't really specific when I asked for a disaster."

Luana couldn't believe her ears.

"Hold on, are you really serious?" she asked. "So this is all true this thing that runs in the family? Like I always know when grandma is going to call or the premonitions I see in my dreams?"

"Well, we are shamans from father to son and even from mother to daughter, whether you want it or not. You could become one, Luana. But you don't have to develop your gift if you don't want to. Only you can decide."

"No thanks, Miguel, I think I would become crazy.

And I don't want to spend my time curing people like you. It's not my thing."

"You'll see. You will always be welcome here if you change your mind."

I had put my head into my hands. I was condemned. I knew it. Everything I had felt was real. The feeling of being strangled. The curse was real and I had no choice. If I wanted to get rid of it, I would have to face it at the price of an unknown catastrophe and a potentially deadly one for me. Or I should give up on holidays my entire life for fear of losing all my boyfriends.

But any serious boyfriend would be bound to ask me to go on holiday at some point and…this curse had been ruining my life for fourteen years and if as Miguel said, there was no other way, then I was prepared to face my destiny. When we said goodbye to Miguel, I asked him a last question:

"And if I kissed you right now, since you were the one who cast the spell, wouldn't it cancel it?"

"Well, first I don't think my wife would appreciate it, and then, that wouldn't change a thing. A curse is a curse. You must face it or bear it your entire life. I'm really sorry Julia. I know it will take some courage."

He took me in his strong arms and I felt a certain attraction between us in the way he held me.

"Goodbye, Julia."

And to think that I could have ended the curse right then and there if he hadn't been married! What could have happened in his home? Furthermore as a shaman, I'm sure he would have found a way to protect us.

Luana couldn't believe all these revelations. She

started telling me about strange stories that had happened in her family and there were tons. It was scary.

"In your dreams, did you ever see a catastrophe involving me?" I asked.

"No, but I saw a black cat in my dream last night."

"Don't say that. Now I've become extremely superstitious. Let's hope it won't be that bad."

The rest of the holiday in Mexico did me good. I needed a change of air after witnessing the jealousy scenes of my ex, Charlie, who begged me to go back to him, even though I had left him more than a month before this trip. He really annoyed me.

I was amazed by all that I was seeing during this road trip. We had rented a car and we drove in turn without really respecting the speed limits on windy mountain roads. We were playing with death. Especially me. As if I wanted to prepare for this catastrophe.

The scenery was breathtaking: the Mayas' sacred sites, the muscular men who dived from the cliffs of Acapulco, the *voladores* who were spinning in the void to make the rain come…

But the curse carried on throughout the entire holiday. First I needed to find a man I liked, which wasn't that easy. As always, Luana had found a boyfriend, Gabriel, and I remained alone. On the last night, a guy had come to me at the beach bar where we were hanging in Puerto Escondido. He looked like a surfer. Lots of muscles, tanned and a jaw a little too square for my taste but he was quite cute nevertheless with his blue eyes and his brown hair.

When I saw him come close, I thought it would be an

opportunity to end so many years of frustrated holiday romance and aborted long relationships as well as this damned curse! He wasn't so much to my liking, but I was open to anything to end the curse. And what could happen? A tsunami? A storm? The bar catching fire? Everything was calm, I didn't see any imminent risk. He came in my direction and talked to me with a strong Texan accent:

"Hey, I'm Andy, what's your name?"

"Hi, I'm Julia."

"Oh, you're French, aren't you?"

"Yes. What about you?"

"American, I come from Dallas. Are you on vacation here?"

"Yes, with my friend Luana."

I pointed him to her and he stared at her from head to toe. Luana is a gorgeous woman. She waved at him. I carried on with the introductions:

"And her boyfriend Gabriel."

Andy briefly pulled a face before smiling broadly. Maybe his dreams of threesome for the night had just vanished. Gabriel shook his hand.

"Hi."

Then Andy leant closer to my ears and whispered:

"What would you say if we vanished just the two of us… We could go to my hotel room…"

Men had come on strong to me before, but this time I couldn't believe my ears. This man was an artist! Three sentences and straight to the goal! This was my moment! I was about to answer, when I saw in the corner of my eye a furious girl coming straight towards Andy. She seemed drunk. She caught him by the arm and started talking to him.

"Oh there you are! So that's how you treat your conquests? You spend the night with them and then when you got what you needed you throw them away? I waited a whole hour for you today and you never came! And here I find you hitting on the first girl you see…"

Andy said nothing. Maybe he waited for her to finish? As for me, I could see that the curse was unfolding before my eyes once more. As always when I was about to kiss a guy, there was always something preventing it. Fourteen years of mysterious coincidences had started to really drive me insane. The girl didn't stop:

"You used me! You said it was love at first sight and I was foolish enough to believe you!"

The girl had raised her voice so that everyone would hear her.

"May I have your attention girls! This guy is an unstoppable seducer who is going to take advantage of you and leave you the morning after!"

Andy looked really embarrassed. He didn't know what to do. In the end he took her by the arm.

"Let's go talk in private, shall we?"

She looked at him a little disconcerted. They walked further down the beach. My last chance to break the curse before the end of our stay had just vanished. I was tired and I left Luana and Gabriel to kiss on the beach, while I went back to the hotel. Once more disillusioned to have let my luck pass by, I watched Gabriel and Luana say goodbye before we hit the road again.

We drove to the airport and I thought everything was

over. Maybe frustration pushes us to do crazy things… Or was it the will to stop the curse once and for all?

CHAPTER 3
ON THE MEXICO-PARIS PLANE

In the boarding queue, I checked around me one last time in case there was any attractive man; but just like on the outbound flight, I saw no one. I accepted the fact the curse wouldn't be conjured this time and I found solace in the idea that I would have to go on holiday real soon again. Unless I picked a random man on the plane. I was looking feverishly around me. It was my last chance to break the curse. I couldn't care less if that meant a plane crash!

We didn't get great seats on the flight: we were stuck in the central aisle, which had four seats. We had ended up with the two seats in the middle, which meant that we always had to disturb the people sitting next to us if we wanted to get up. The woman next to me seemed to be about the same age as us, while the man next to Luana looked like he was about fifty years old. I cast a quick look at him, but wasn't that desperate to end the curse with that man!

Once settled in, I finally saw a man who attracted me. He was sitting one row further up on the right aisle. I hadn't seen him in the queue earlier. Maybe he had arrived late?

I could only see him from the side. He had brown hair,

fair skin and I could see small wrinkles at the corner of his eyes. I guessed he was a little bit older than me, maybe between five and ten years. He was wearing an elegant suit and it was the first really attractive man I had seen in three weeks. Another man in a suit, which was too small for him was sitting next to him. They were talking together and I thought that they must be colleagues. He seemed much less cute, but I couldn't really distinguish his features from where I was sitting. I gave Luana a nudge.

"Look!"

With my eyes, I pointed to where the guy was sitting.

"What?"

"The guy in a suit in the next row up from us."

She watched him discreetly and pulled a face.

"Not bad but a bit old, maybe?"

"No, he must be something like 35, 36 years old?"

I was a bit disappointed by her lack of enthusiasm.

"You think so?" she answered, more interested by the magazine on her knees.

"In any case, it's the first attractive man I've seen since the beginning of our trip. So what do we do?"

"You mean, what do you do? I'm not doing anything..."

It was my chance to break the curse that had been poisoning my life for years. I looked at her imploringly.

"But I can't go and talk to him like that."

"Why not?"

"A girl doesn't do that."

"If you like him, then, yes, a girl does do that."

"But I don't dare."

"Then forget it."

I cried:

"But it's easy for you to say, you got Gabriel and you don't have a damned curse on you!"

"And so what? It's not like I've had a holiday romance every time I was on vacation!"

"What are you talking about Luana? Every time we go on holiday together, I'm always the one who comes back with no love story to tell."

Luana buckled her belt.

"Really? I never noticed…"

The worst thing was that, she was being sincere… I raised my eyes to heaven as I buckled my belt too.

"Did you really never notice? Our holiday in the South of France? The one in Barcelona? And when we went to Ischia? Nothing! *Nada*! Whereas you always found a holiday lover. The only time you didn't have one is because you were crazy about Edouard who had to stay in Paris. And even then I didn't find anyone!"

"Now you say it… I bring you bad luck, don't I? If that's what you think, we can stop going on holiday together."

"Stop being a fool! It's your cousin who brought me this bad luck. I only need to find a way to speak to the guy in the next row. If you help me, maybe it will be the end of the curse."

Luana shook her head:

"For your guy over there, it's simple, you just need to go talk to him."

"I told you, I'm too scared! I don't know him."

Luana thought for a moment.

"Ok, then there is another way. Less… Head-on… If you want…"

Luana dug a pen and paper out of her bag and handed it to me:

"Now you're on! Write something on this piece of paper and ask the woman next to you to pass it on to him. If he's interested, he will answer, if not, then you'll have tried, you'll have no regrets and we can watch a good movie instead!"

I shook my head.

"No, sorry, I don't want to."

The woman next to me, who apparently had eavesdropped on our conversation told us:

"No problem, girls. If you write it, I'll pass it on."

I stared at her, speechless.

"Are you sure?" I said.

She answered by clapping her hands together in excitement:

"But of course! I fly from Paris to Mexico all the time for work and I've never seen anything as exciting on a plane. I hope he will reply!"

Luana nudged me.

"You see. Even she agrees!"

I shrugged.

"But what do I write? I have no idea. And if he only speaks Spanish? What do I do? I won't spend the evening improvising in sign language…"

Luana started to show signs of impatience.

"If it's the case, I will translate. And to kiss a guy, you don't need to talk, do you? In any case, I'm sure he's a business man and speaks English."

"Do you think so? But I still don't know what to begin with."

"Maybe by writing *Hello* in several languages? And he will answer in the language he wants?"

"Well thought."

I asked Luana the spelling of *Hello, my name is Julia. What's yours?* in Spanish. Then, I grasped the pen and paper and started to write.

Salut, Buongiorno, Hello, Buenas Tardes, Guten Tag! Je m'appelle Julia. Mi chiamo Julia. My name is Julia. Me llamo Julia. Ich heisse Julia. Et toi ? E tu? And you? Y usted? Und dich?

I showed my work to Luana.

"Perfect! Now fold it and let's pass it on!"

I hesitated.

"No, not yet. Maybe after take-off."

Luana folded the paper I gave her to read it.

"Come on, what are you waiting for? It's a twelve hour flight. If nothing interesting happens, then we can watch a few good films! We might as well know now."

I took back the paper in my hands.

"Wait! It's not a good idea. This curse won't end this way... Especially when your cousin predicted a big catastrophe if I find a holiday lover. What if the plane crashes by my fault?"

Luana tried to take the paper out of my hands.

"Shut up about the curse, I'm sure my cousin exaggerated the whole thing."

The paper fell on the floor and the woman next to me

leant down to pick it up before I could stop her and knocked on the guy's shoulder one row up. He turned, surprised. I could see him better. He looked a little older than I thought. Maybe 35-40 years old. She pointed at me when she gave him the paper. I smiled to him, blushing. When he unfolded the paper and started to read it, I wanted to dig a hole and hide in it. I cast an accusing look at Luana who was laughing like mad.

"Hey but why are you staring at me this way? You wanted to know if he was attracted to you, didn't you? Later you will thank me…"

I wasn't totally convinced and I turned towards the woman next to me. There was a hint of accusation in my tone.

"Thank you, but there was no emergency."

She responded to cool things down:

"Sorry, but I couldn't resist seeing something interesting finally take place on a Mexico-Paris flight. If you had waited any longer, you may have changed your mind."

I didn't have time to answer before the guy one row up passed the same piece of paper back to my neighbour, who in turn, gave it to me. I opened it with apprehension. Luana and the woman next to me leant in to read it too. It was written in French."

Hi, my name is Eric. You speak French?

Fantastic! Not only did he reply, but he was French like me. Could this be the end of the curse? Luana clapped her hands together thrilled with excitement.

"You see, he did reply! Thanks Madam, if you had done nothing, Julia would still be here hesitating."

Luana shook my neighbour's hand.

"Yes, but I'm going to work when we land, so I need to sleep straight after dinner."

She pointed at a box of sleeping pills.

"So if you want to exchange any other love notes, it's now or never! After that you will have to deal with it by yourself."

I looked at her incredulous.

"Sorry to curb your enthusiasm, but this is all going a little too quick for me. What do I say? I have no idea what to do next…"

Luana rolled her eyes.

"Hello, yes, I'm French from Paris, what about you? Since when is it so difficult to have a conversation, Julia?"

Luana was right. Normally I wasn't shy and I had no problems to spark up a conversation, but here I was faced with an unusual situation. I had no idea how things would evolve and I was beginning to feel stressed. And I knew nothing about him. I was jumping into the unknown. I wrote.

My name is Julia, I'm French from Paris. What about you?

The woman next to me asked when I had finished writing.

"So now can I give it to him?"

I gave her the folded paper.

The plane took off. The woman next to me had given the piece of paper to Eric. I was trying to concentrate on my fear of dying on a plane that I always had when planes took off and landed instead of thinking about dying of shame after having initiated this dangerous game.

Why did I ever point out this guy to Luana? And how did I end up sitting next to such an enterprising neighbour? Damned curse, really made me go out of my comfort zone to conjure it. If this little game excited my neighbor so much, why didn't she write to strangers in planes?

When I observed her, I understood why. She wore a ring on her left hand. She was married, but probably felt excited by the idea of reliving what belonged to an almost adolescent age by proxys... Because yes, that was exactly it. A teenager's game based on a plane instead of a classroom. Even if I didn't remember ever sending love notes in class.

Eric had written something down, then gave back the paper to the woman next to me. That meant he was interested. Maybe the game wasn't that bad after all... I unfolded the paper that my neighbor handed to me with a knowing smile. The eyes of Luana and the woman next to me were fixated on it as if what was written on it contained the Secret of Creation. I read.

> I'm from Bordeaux. I'm on my way back from a business trip with my colleague. What about you? What were you doing in Mexico?

I didn't know what to say. The truth? Or invent a character to spark his curiosity? Maybe I shouldn't have revealed my identity? I should have thought more and taken another one to protect myself. What if he harassed me? I didn't know anything about him, or so little... Why the hell did I give him my real name? I looked at him chatting to his colleague and I wasn't so sure I wanted to carry on playing. It was all a mistake.

My anguished thoughts were interrupted by the steward, who wanted to know what I wanted to drink. Behind him, I could see Eric was watching me and when the steward gave me a glass of water, he raised his glass too displaying an irresistible smile. I blushed while he lowered his eyes and turned to talk to his colleague.

I was troubled by his smile and also by the fact he carried on talking without realising the shame his gesture caused me. It was time to find something to reply. My heart was beating so fast. I was both excited and worried about having to talk to him. For now I felt protected. I was not ready for a conversation yet. It was a bit like when you exchange messages on a dating website before meeting for a drink. You feel you can say a lot of things, even very intimate things, because you're protected by the screen in between. I wrote.

I was in Mexico with my friend for a holiday...

I had folded the paper to pass it on to him when Luana frowned.

"But you can't give it like that. You need to ask a question, or else the conversation will end. Do you want something to happen or not?"

"I don't know! What if this guy was crazy or totally dumb. What if he forced me into something I didn't want?"

"So what? I will defend you: if he gets too close, I will give him a punch he will remember!"

Luana started to pretend punching in the air and then stopped. I stared at her smiling.

"I don't think he will do anything to you on this plane. You only have to yell for people to come and rescue you. But if you want something to happen, ask him to exchange seats. I can go next to his colleague and you can talk freely."

"Are you sure?"

Luana held her head higher to spot Eric's colleague and made a disgusted face.

"Er... yes. It's a shame that his colleague is not cuter. But at least, his shoulder looks comfortable, I should be able to have a good nap."

I looked at Luana with big eyes. This girl would never cease to amaze me.

"Come on, ask him and after dinner, we'll swap seats."

I nodded and wrote.

What do you say if we swapped seats? My friend can take yours and you can come next to me, so that we can have a chat?

Once I finished writing, I smiled at the woman next to me who took the paper with an assured gesture, ready to fulfill her official love note passer mission…

"Thanks."

She smiled.

"You're welcome, but it's the last time I pass it on. After that, you're on your own."

I nodded.

"So be it..." I whispered for myself.

The steward was handing out meals. While I was eating, I prepared for what I was going to say. What if he was boring? Or worse, what if he said nothing? Maybe I wouldn't find him that attractive from close-up? Mmmh, he was from Bordeaux. I had never been there, maybe that could be something to talk about? No, what was I thinking? I was chewing nervously, trying not to panic. All of a sudden, I had an idea.

"Luana, maybe it would be better if I went and talked to him before you guys switch seats."

Luana shrugged:

"Whatever..."

"I was thinking I could pretend I'm going to the bathroom so I can talk to him on my way."

"Good idea! But have a piece of chewing-gum before you go please, otherwise your chicken guacamole breath will kill him before you even start talking."

Luana took a pack of chewing-gum out of her bag.

"Here, take one!"

I smelt my breath.

"Oh my God, you're right! Oh damn. It's double or quits now. I'm going. Or rather... No. What should I say to him?"

Luana sighed, a little exasperated by my indecision.

"Hey, I'm Julia, the girl who wrote you the little notes. Would that do?"

"This part I can deal with. But after? What do I tell him?"

"I don't know... Talk about the trip. Ask him how he

found Mexico? If he comes often? Ask him about his work. And if he's interesting, ask him to come and sit next to you. If not, you can always say that you're actually quite tired and you need to sleep. And I'm here if need be."

"Ok, ok, I will take my courage in both hands and go talk to Mister sexy."

Luana put her thumbs up.

"That's how I like you. Good luck!"

I extracted myself out of my seat trying to dodge the woman next to me. I took a long breath to try and calm myself down. It felt like my heart was beating at thousand miles an hour and seemed to explode in my chest. I straightened my clothes in the corridor and took a step towards Eric.

"Hi, I'm Julia."

At last I looked at him in the eyes, but I couldn't hold his gaze for a long time. His smile had broadened as soon as he had seen me. I held my hand towards him, but instead of shaking it, he got up and kissed me on each cheek the French way. While kissing me, he remained a little longer than the usual on my cheeks and I kind of liked that first physical contact. For sure, I hadn't been mistaken. I was really attracted to Eric. It was a relief because until then I had only seen him from a distance and from the side. I thought of the number of times when I had clocked someone from afar in a party, thought he was cute and while getting closer, realized my mistake.

"Ah here you are finally! I'm glad to meet you. I'm Eric. But you know that already…"

He had a quite strong Southern accent and a deep voice

that made him all the sexier.

"And here's my colleague, Louis."

Louis wanted to get up too to kiss me, but his head hit the ceiling. So he sat down massaging his head with one hand and holding the other to shake mine.

"Nice to meet you."

"Nice to meet you too", I answered.

I dived deep into Eric's gaze again but found nothing more interesting to say than:

"So are you getting ready to sleep?"

"No, we were going to watch a movie. Maybe we can negotiate with Louis' neighbor so you can join us, if you want."

I pointed towards Luana.

"Well, I was thinking that my friend Luana could swap her seat with yours, Louis, so we can talk a bit before watching a movie if you agree, of course!"

Eric exchanged a glance with Louis who agreed.

"Yes, no worries!" he said.

"Perfect! I'll be back in a second and then we can switch."

In the little time that that conversation had lasted, I could see Eric from closer up. He hadn't stopped smiling and I kind of liked him. But I had a weird feeling that a danger was looming. He was cute, but normally I wouldn't have gone for someone older than me. He had little wrinkles at the corner of his eyes and we were probably about ten or fifteen years apart.

If it weren't to stop the curse, I would never have found the courage to use such a crazy strategy, I had to admit. The Mexico-Paris flight was my last chance to do something extraordinary... Maybe to live out a fantasy too? I had never had sex on a plane before. At the simple thought of this possibility, my senses started to awaken. Now the dice had been thrown. Anything could happen. And I had all the cards in my hand to win this game. Unless this damned curse prevented me from kissing him once again.

While I was waiting in line to get into the bathroom, I observed the coming and going of stewards and stewardesses: their meeting point was right next to the toilets and there was always one of them around. If I wanted anything to happen, I would need to be cunning. Maybe later, when everyone would be sleeping including the flight attendants?

Finally the toilet door in front of me opened. It was my turn to get in. I entered the "fantasy" cabin, which seemed so exciting to me a minute ago. But I had to admit what it was in reality: a disgusting place! Hundreds of people must have used it already and we were only at the beginning of the trip. The cleanliness of the place was already dubious. Furthermore, it was ridiculously small. You'd have to be an acrobat to be able to kiss in there…

I looked at myself in the mirror and it sent back the reflection of a slightly tanned girl in tight jeans and an adjusted t-shirt, a casual scarf resting elegantly on the neckline. I winked at myself.

"Yes, my dear Julia, he won't be able to resist you!"

As a matter of fact, I was saying that to give myself courage more than anything. What I always lacked was confidence. I knew girls who weren't that beautiful, but who were sure of themselves. And that attitude attracted men like magnets. And why the hell couldn't I be like them? Maybe I didn't feel beautiful enough or in a different league? I watched my reflection in the mirror.

"Look me in the eyes, Julia: tonight you will be self-assurance personified."

I tried to convince myself as much as I could. The opportunity was just too perfect. It was a chance to re-boost my ego too. Finally someone had chosen to play with me, the game had begun and I had to play my trump cards. The fact that I had started the game had earned me a head start. Now I had to see what his next move would be…

I wished myself luck, while casting one last look at myself to be sure I was ready. I didn't know how this story was going to end, but at least it was pretty exciting!

There! I had materialised in front of Eric with my prettiest smile and the most sensual voice possible. I said:

"So are you ready to swap places?"

"With pleasure!" he answered with his chanting accent.

I turned towards his colleague.

"Good night, Louis. I'm sending you Luana in a second…"

I made a gesture inviting Eric to follow me. The woman next to me and Luana had spied on me all this time hoping that I wouldn't notice.

"And here's Luana!, I said, pointing at her."

Eric looked at her as if he was admiring a painting. His smile was too broad for my liking... Jealousy invaded me. Then, I remembered what I had told myself in front of the mirror.

Jealous people are not confident in themselves. And I didn't want to be that kind of person. Only a confident one. It was easier said than done! It wasn't because I had decided it that all of a sudden I had transformed into a woman perfectly sure of herself. *Fake it 'til you make it* they say. I tried to find reassurance in the fact that Eric was there for me. Even though I hoped the curse wouldn't rear its head once more in the form of Eric falling head over heels with Luana or even the woman next to me!

"Nice to meet you, Luana," he said.

Luana held her hand, just nearly avoiding to knock her head on the ceiling:

"Nice to meet you too. So do you want me to go and sit next to your neighbour?"

"Yes, if that's not too much trouble," I said.

"Not at all... Have fun. I'm going to sleep, I'm exhausted!"

I waved goodbye at her while she got herself out of her seat and paced towards Louis.

Finally, I got back to my seat next to my neighbour, who pretended she was sleeping. I was pretty sure she wouldn't miss out on the opportunity to eavesdrop on our conversation. Eric took the seat next to me, the fifty years old guy next to him. He didn't seem too happy on the changeover. Eric leant over my ear and whispered on a very sensual tone.

"So, what do we do now?"

I was so surprised by this change of voice, that I answered almost inaudibly.

"Let's talk a bit, get to know each other…"

"All right, then if you allow me, I'm dying to ask… Do

you often write to strangers on planes?"

I laughed nervously.

"No, to tell the truth, it's my first time. What about you? Do you often reply to notes from strangers?"

He laughed.

"No, for me too it's a first! But how did you get this idea?"

"Well, it's not mine, but Luana's."

"What do you mean?"

I decided to tell the truth.

"She saw I liked you, but I would never dare to talk to you. So she thought up this strategy. Let's say she just helped me a bit…"

He laughed again.

"I think she did well."

I answered uncertain.

"You think?"

"But of course! I would have spent the flight talking to Louis, or maybe watching a movie, or sleeping. Luckily a cute young woman has shaken things up a little…"

I blushed. Did I just dream, or did he just say I was cute? I wasn't really at ease with compliments.

"Oh... Thanks!" I said, trying to find a subject of conversation. "Don't you get on with your colleague?"

"Oh, he's nice, he tells the best jokes ever. But he's a colleague, full stop. Not a friend."

"I understand. So you were on a business trip… Were you able to get away and have some time for yourself?"

"No, not really. We worked long hours and we were only there for five days. With the jet-lag, I only slept, worked and all I got to see of Mexico was very good food:

Chili con carne, Tacos, Nachos, Fajitas, Enchiladas, etc. I must have put on a kilo with every meal... It was my first time in Mexico. I wish I could have seen the sights, but that will be for another time."

"You have to go back. The country is magnificent: the Mayas ruins are incredible, the landscapes, the beaches…"

He took my hand and whispered sensually:

"Maybe I could go back with you. You'd be my guide."

I withdrew my hand quickly. Everything was going too fast. I needed to know him a bit more, before things get a little more intimate... But I had made the first step, so he must have felt that the coast was clear for him.

"Maybe. But the real guide is my friend Luana. She's Mexican and speaks Spanish. I can understand some of it, but speaking it is another story. Do you speak it yourself?"

Eric whispered:

"Yes. And I can do so many more things with my tongue…"

The least I could say, was that Eric went straight to the point. Things were speeding up dangerously and I felt like I was trapped into a vicious cycle without knowing where it would end. His reaction left me speechless for a moment. I should never have answered the following:

"Oh yes?"

Eric glanced on the side. He was looking at his colleague. Louis was already fast asleep and so was Luana leaning on his shoulder. Eric turned towards me and without letting me breathe, he drew me towards him, and…I received a violent nudge from my neighbour who had turned towards me in her sleep. I suppressed a:

"Ouch!"

"Are you all right?" asked Eric, visibly worried.

"Yes, I'm going to be fine," I said.

I started massaging my sore back. The woman next to me seemed to be sleeping blissfully and hadn't realised what she had done. I couldn't help but thinking that again, the curse was going to prevent anything from happening. I was expecting any moment that Eric would vomit his chicken guacamole on me. Or even worse, that the fifty years old guy next to Eric was a terrorist about to threaten to kill everyone on board.

"Would you like me to massage you where she hit you?"

And without waiting for my response, Eric put his hand on my waist under my t-shirt and started to massage my skin slowly. His contact electrified my entire body. He put his other hand under my chin to get my face closer to his and kissed me impulsively with unsuspected passion. I responded to his ardor with even more impetuosity. He kissed like a god. It was as if two lonely people had found one another. I was surprised by such intensity. All of a sudden I realised the curse was lifted. At the very last minute, it's true, but still… I had had my holiday romance finally, after years of forced celibacy.

I caught my breath. Eyes shut, I was expecting to hear the engine explode any time, pass through an air hole or be struck by lightning. But nothing happened. I was alive, no catastrophe seemed to have happened. Luana was right, it may not be so serious after all. Freed from that weight, I gave myself completely to that fiery kiss.

Until a doubt came into my mind. What if the plane didn't count? After all it was the traveling part, not exactly the holiday one. Did I really lift the curse? Plus, there was always a moment where the man escaped me. This time it went all too easily. He didn't get sick when he kissed me, me neither. No snake on the plane or turbulences. Just a little nudge from my neighbour. Oh, after all, who cared? Eric kissed divinely well...

"I must say you're right, you are an expert with your tongue."

Eric smiled.

"You haven't seen anything yet..."

I didn't want to know what he was alluding to or rather I did. What was sure is that he didn't leave me time to reflect. He took my mouth again without me giving him permission and devoured it with ferocious ardour. It was as if he was fresh out of prison and hadn't had contact with a woman for years. Maybe it was the case? I hadn't asked anything about his past love life... If he had been single for a long time, for example... I only assumed that if he replied to my messages, then surely he was single. Or else why would he do this?

We had put the blankets over us and he started to put his hands under my clothes. Everything was going fast, much too fast for my taste. I had initiated this game and I could not go backwards. I wish I had spent more time chatting with him, getting to know him... But the love notes had made it clear to him that I was free and willing, and sitting so close to each other had done the rest.

Even though I was left distraught by the turn of events,

I still found the situation exciting. The more I looked at Eric and the more I was attracted to him. And the way he kissed and touched me started to drive me crazy. I let him touch me while trying to remain the most discreet as possible, helped by the fact that our neighbours were asleep or at least pretended to be. Here and there, the light from flat screens interrupted the monotony of the countless blankets over night masks.

There were no flight attendants in sight. Eric took my face in his hand and whispered.

"You seem worried…"

He kissed me with the same feverish intensity and took my hand under the blanket. He guided it under his shirt. I could feel his sculpted abs and started to caress his torso. But his hand still resting on mine wanted me to go elsewhere. I withdrew it and whispered in his ear.

"No, not here."

"Ok, then where else?"

"Where?"

"There are not thousands of places to go on a plane. The only challenge is avoiding that the flight attendants see us."

I glanced furtively in the corridor. Everybody seemed asleep.

"The coast is clear."

On the one hand I wanted him badly, which was fueled by wanting to do something forbidden. On the other hand I was panicked at the idea of giving myself to a guy I barely knew. Eric didn't leave me room to ask myself too many questions.

"Go to the left. I'm going to go the other side. Get into

one of the toilets but don't lock the door. I'll come right after, so it doesn't look suspicious. I'll make sure the flight attendants don't see us and then I'll come inside."

"And what if someone is watching?"

"You'll have to wait a bit."

I was about to climb over my neighbor but I changed my mind.

"Wouldn't it be easier if we both got up on the same side so we don't wake up both our neighbors?"

"You're right, let's get up on my side."

"Ok."

I tried as much as I could to get out of my seat without disturbing the fifty year old man, but without success. I climbed over and of course woke him up. He looked at me as if I were a prostitute and groaned heavily to show his discomfort.

While going up the aisle, I thought about how crazy I was. And at the same time, I felt so free from the curse that I wanted to celebrate. When I got into one of the toilets, I realised once more how tiny it would be for two people. And the worst part was, it was in an even more disgusting state than before. There was water everywhere, especially in the sink where the person before me had left white stuff floating in the water... It was something I couldn't really identify: toothpaste, spit, or…

I sighed, disgusted. There was no going back anyway. Any moment now, Eric would open the door. I started to empty the water in the sink. I started regretting the whole idea. It was really not a nice place for holiday romance. I had imagined something much more romantic.

I reassured myself with the fact that the curse was

behind me and I was still alive. I had finished emptying the sink when the door opened. I stood on the toilets to let Eric come in but had to crouch as the height in there didn't allow me to. It was the only way to close the door, which wasn't that easy. Eric finally managed to lock it.

I looked at Eric interogatively.

"Did they see you come in?"

"No, I don't think so. But there's a lady next door who gave me a right stare when she saw you inside."

"Whatever... Where were we at?"

I was stunned by my audacity and was all the more surprised by his. I was still crouching on the toilets. He held his hand to help me get down. I found myself in his arms, my legs around his waist: there was no way two people could fit in this place without being tightly bound. I squeezed his waist with all my strength so I didn't fall. He put his lips onto mine kissing me in the same savage way he had started earlier. I was feeling an urgent desire for him. My entire body was telling me that the wait had been way too long. His hands were going along my spine, while I was caressing his hair and that he deepened our kiss even more. All of a sudden he stopped.

"Julia, can you get back on the seat please?"

"Yes, of course..."

Was I too heavy? It was too beautiful, everything was going far too smoothly for someone affected by a curse. He put his two hands on my trousers, ready to unbutton them.

"Can I?"

It was more a rhetorical question than anything. He left it on the hook and started to kiss my belly. Then he grabbed my pants and put them down in one go. He helped me get rid of them and I felt his tongue go down from my belly button.

"Help me put your legs around my neck and hold on to anything you can higher up."

I felt like Victoria Abril in Pedro Almodovar's High Heels. My body was doing everything Eric wanted. I wasn't thinking anymore. I was at his mercy. I was holding the tissue dispenser with one hand and hanging to his neck with the other, while Eric was absorbed by his task. I closed my eyes... My body started moving with him. My mind transported me onto the beach of Puerto Escondido. I could see myself naked, lying onto an isolated lounge chair.

I came back to reality. I was so afraid that we could be heard from the other side of the plane or be exposed. At the same time, danger fueled my arousal. The strength of my pleasure surprised me. I didn't know where I was anymore and I bit my hand not to scream. I had never known an orgasm so intense. When I recovered myself and finally opened my eyes, he looked at me and said:

"Again?"

I couldn't believe my ears. I could have said yes, but I was still a bit dazed and confused from what just happened. It was something brand new for me. I realised he was still totally dressed. I hadn't even seen his body.

"Help me get back onto the seat." I asked.

It was comical, I almost fell several times. Once on it I could crouch and I started to kiss him while I put my hand under his t-shirt. I stroked his back and then grabbed his t-shirt to take it off. He didn't protest. My hands remained on his torso, while I was still kissing him. I didn't see how we could make love in there. Straddling him was going to be tricky. I was going to bang my head everywhere. And all of a sudden I realised. Shit!!!

"Do you have what it takes?"

He unbuttoned his trousers and put his pants down.

"I think so, yes, what do you reckon?"

"No, I meant, do you have condoms?"

He laughed.

"Yes, of course, don't worry."

He took his wallet out of his trouser pockets and took one out that he gave to me.

"Ladies first."

I tore off the packaging and put the thing on.

"There's only one way to make love in here," he said.

"Which is?"

"Get closer to me."

"Well there aren't many other options…"

He laughed. I put my hands around his neck to kiss him and I helped him into position. I did as asked. I held onto him the best I could…

***

I was back sitting next to Eric in the plane. The situation felt strange now, as if we had come back to reason after a moment of craziness. Only some sort of shame lingered on now. He was saying nothing. And the feeling was getting worse.

In truth, I wanted to be alone. When I had left the toilets, a steward had looked at me with a mocking air, after he realised there was a man hiding behind me. I had hurried up to get back to my seat next to the neighbour who had passed on the love notes and who I had now woken up unintentionally. She opened her eyes and said:

"So? Did it work?"

"Yes."

"Awesome!"

Eric was going down the aisle. The woman next to me pretended she was asleep. Eric woke up the other neighbour, who must have totally hated us by now, as he tried to get back into his seat. Then once settled in, he leant onto my ear to tell me softly:

"I'm going to try and sleep, what about you?"

"Me too. I'm exhausted."

"Ok. Good night."

Was that it? After this moment of craziness, I was expecting a hug or a nice chat before getting to sleep. I kissed him one last time, but this time the fire of passion had gone. He gave me one of the most chaste kisses, which contrasted completely with the ones he had given me about five minutes before. I didn't know what to think. I put it down to tiredness and tried to find a comfortable position under my blanket.

"May I put my head on your shoulder?"

"Yes, of course."

That wasn't the best idea. Even when using the little cushion the company was graciously providing, his shoulder wasn't the most comfortable. Usually I could never sleep in a plane. I knew the only proven way to get through that trip: a sleeping pill.

I now bitterly regretted, not having brought one with

me, when I saw how cold towards me Eric turned. Maybe he really felt like sleeping? Which I could understand. But something felt odd in the way he was so quick to say goodnight. He was now treating me as if we were friends, not lovers. Even his kiss good night was strange. It was as if, between the moment he had left the toilets and the moment he came back to sit next to me, he was a different man. Cold, ice-cold even. There were seven hours to go and I was afraid they would prove very long.

I thought of what just happened. And I didn't know what to make of it. Yes, the situation had been exciting. And Eric had brought me to heights of ecstasy like no man before. But in seven hours' time, would there be anything left between us? Already his need to sleep had taken the spark out of our encounter. I would have talked with him all night long. But things had got out of control and even if, at the moment, I had gone with the flow, doubts invaded me now that I was in the calm of my own thoughts.

I had been so focused on the holiday romance story because of the curse. But in reality, I was looking for true love. I had promised myself not to ever go out with a man like Charlie again, my ex. A man I could never really fall in love with, probably because he snored. But I had wanted to challenge the curse. I didn't want to go home without having a holiday romance even if I knew it wouldn't really last. I know I'm contradictory.

So I did go crazy earlier and now I didn't know where to hide anymore. Yes, that man had seemed terribly attractive, but hadn't we been in that place, this adventure would never have happened.

He was older. And I was usually attracted to men my age or younger. In the haste of the moment, I had forgotten to ask him how old he was. I didn't know much about him, yet I was unsuccessfully trying to sleep on his shoulder.

I decided to wait for him to be asleep to watch a movie. I didn't want to dwell on what had happened. I just wanted to get out of this plane and go home. And forget about all of this and pretend it was a dream. I didn't want him to kiss me when he woke up after what had just happened. I hoped that when they would serve breakfast, he would get back to his seat next to his colleague and Luana next to me.

Luana! She was still asleep on Louis' shoulder, lucky girl! After I had checked Eric was sleeping too, I had found a French-subtitled Mexican movie and I started watching it. I must have finally fallen asleep because I couldn't remember seeing more than twenty minutes of it. I had woken up as breakfast was being served. I turned my head towards Eric and opened my eyes. He smiled at me.

"Hi."

"Hmmm, hi," I said, stretching my arms.

The episode of yesterday came back.

"I think it would be better if I went back to my seat."

The coldness of our last exchange was still lingering apparently.

"Ah, and I would appreciate if you could keep quiet about what happened between us. I have a wife and two children and I don't want my colleague to know about our little affair."

While he was telling me this, he put his wedding ring back onto his finger. I was so shocked that I nodded without being able to utter a word. He didn't leave me time to do that anyway. He got up, climbed over me and the woman next to me without waking her up. Then I saw him wake Luana up and go back to his seat.

I had been with a married man! I had violated all my rules in one night! Usually I always avoided men that were already in a relationship. It was only a source of problems. Worst: he had taken advantage of the situation. Was I the only one he had had an affair with or was he used to this sort of thing? I didn't know and I didn't want to know. Or maybe I did. A little...

Luana had come back to her seat in the meantime. She was all smiles, but when she saw my sombre face, she gave me a questioning look.

"Now, tell me everything!"

"It's worse than you think..."

"What happened?"

"I should have never written those love notes."

"But why?"

"He used me."

"What? How?"

"We talked together, and then very quickly we kissed. Then we went off to the toilet cubicle and then we... Well you can guess what happened next. When he got back to our seats, he casually said good night and suddenly became very cold. I found this odd, the way he wanted to sleep right away. I thought we would talk all night long... And when he woke up this morning, he asked me to keep quiet about it because he didn't want his colleague to know what happened between us. He's married and he didn't tell me anything! Can you believe it? I did to another woman, what I would never want anyone to do to me..."

"But that's horrible!"

"I've been tricked. And to say I was totally under his charm... I'm sure he must be wondering if I'm going to make a scene before we get off the plane."

"Let me think. He can't get off this plane thinking his acts won't have consequences!"

"What are you thinking?"

"Leave it with me."

"What? Are you seriously not going to tell me anything?"

"No."

"Ok, I trust you. I know that revenge is a dish best served cold with you."

I looked surreptitiously into Eric's direction who was talking to his colleague as if nothing happened.

"What about your night?" I asked Luana.

"Louis happens to be a great pillow. So for once, I didn't sleep that bad."

I started to laugh. It was relaxing me a bit after what I lived like a treason.

"At least one of us didn't waste her night! I barely slept, I'm exhausted."

"But now you can say you did it in a plane!"

"Great! With a married bastard who took advantage of the situation. I don't think I can boast about it. Even if..."

"What?"

I whispered:

"It was the best sex I ever had…"

"Well maybe that's the most important after all. That you joined the mile high club… The rest doesn't matter."

"Personally, it did matter to me. But I didn't ask if he was in a relationship, so I guess part of it is my fault too."

The steward arrived with breakfast trays.

"Tea or coffee?"

"Tea, please," I said.

"For me a coffee, thanks," asked Luana.

"And here's a coffee and a tea for the two most beautiful girls in the plane…"

I was surprised that he included me in his compliment. Usually, Luana was always the one being noticed... Was this another sign that the curse was really over? Luana's cousin had told me that disaster would strike if I went out with a man while on holiday. He was right. It wasn't the disaster I had expected, though. All these years, I had imagined thousands of different outcomes. A plane crash was the most obvious one to me. But nothing had prepared me to being manipulated that way.

All of a sudden I thought that it wasn't so much my fault for not asking about his status earlier, but his, for not respecting his wife. I didn't even know she existed fifteen minutes ago. I was mad at him for using me in this way, but I knew that if Luana had decided to take revenge, then it would be in an entertaining way. Like the way she had found to connect me with Eric. Luana gave me a nudge.

"Eat. What are you waiting for?"

"Sorry, I was lost in my thoughts."

"You should be hungry after your feats last night."

"You're right. I could eat a horse."

I started to eat, as I watched Eric from the side. I could only see his profile. He was talking with Louis. My neighbour was still asleep.

There was still an hour to go before I could leave the plane and its suffocating atmosphere. I couldn't wait to get out. I wished I could have a shower straight away to get rid of his smell. I didn't want to remember that he touched me. After the steward had collected the empty trays back together, I went to the toilets taking the opposite corridor to where Eric was sitting. The man next to Luana had made his now usual mad look because I was disturbing him once more.

The first available cubicle was the one where we had been with Eric during the night. Was this the irony of fate? It was even more disgusting than before. Thankfully there was no trace of what had happened earlier. Cold water felt good on my hands. I washed my face and neck with all the soap I could find. I wish I could wash myself entirely, but it wasn't practical in this tiny space. I thought about the long bath I would take when I get home. As I couldn't, I brushed my teeth and redid my make-up. There was no way I was going to show Eric how I was feeling. He had tricked me and I was going to remain stoical until the end. I was curious to see what Luana had in mind.

When I came back to my seat, I took the corridor where Eric was seating. I smiled at him, looking sure of myself on the outside, but also to Louis, his colleague. Eric stared at me apprehensively. As if he was afraid of what my next step would be. I didn't know what Luana had up her sleeve, but I was sure it would be worth the wait. Eric looked puzzled now. I tried to get back to my seat. I was astonished to see that the woman next to me was still asleep event though I was awkwardly climbing over her again.

Luana wanted to watch a movie. I joined her. Even if I found it frustrating that there was only enough time to watch the beginning of a film. I would have done anything to get some fresh air and think of something else other than Eric and how I felt insulted by him. I had asked Luana to choose a comedy. The last thing I wanted to see was a drama. I needed to laugh. She had chosen an American comedy I had never heard of. Maybe it hadn't even been distributed in France. I had never seen any of the actors before. The jokes were pretty lame but that was exactly what I needed. Thanks to the movie, I could forget Eric for a few minutes.

The fasten seatbelt sign flashed and the plane started to descend. I never really felt safe on a plane. I always felt like I was going to die before landing. I was clinging to the armrests and waiting for the butterflies in my stomach to go away. Five minutes later, I was bathed in sweat. It was always like this.

Finally we had landed. Phew, at least we hadn't crashed. The only disaster was that I had been taken advantage of by a married man. The rage was rising in me. I wanted to make a scandal in front of everybody, a little like the girl at the bar with Andy. I wish I could slap him in front of his colleague. I even imagined kicking him in the crotch. He would have deserved it.

It was the time to unfasten our seatbelts and take our hand luggage. Luana's was on Eric and Louis' aisle. Mine was opposite. It was better given the state I was in that he wasn't next to me. I didn't want him to talk to me or touch me ever again. Eric carried on staring at me. When I saw him spying on me, I tried to keep a confident look. Disdainful. Luana gestured me to look into her direction.

She went to Louis and said something in his ear. I couldn't work out what it was. Eric neither apparently, but Louis had blushed. He was completely red-faced. He looked at Luana, then Eric with eyes wide opened. Luana gave him a kiss on the cheek and gestured me to go forward.

CHAPTER 4
EXPLOSIVE NEWS

I was so focused on the situation with Eric I hadn't noticed that we were not moving. Everybody had been standing in the aisles for about ten minutes. In front of me, a woman's mobile phone started to ring:

"Hey, how are you? What do you mean swine flu? What are you taking about? Quarantine? For this flight? But what do you mean? What? No, that's impossible, I need to go to work tomorrow. Two days? But when did this swine flu start?"

While I was listening in on the conversation, I had also turned my phone on again. There was a concert of ringtones on the plane. An unusual cacophony of conversations and shouts. The words "swine flu" were on everyone's lips. Panic had started to spread across the plane. Suddenly, the captain made an announcement.

"Dear Passengers, may I ask for your attention please. We are facing an unusual situation. While we were airborne, a violent outbreak of swine flu was reported in Mexico City. Some people could not be helped and died. In most cases swine flu is no more serious than a common winter flu, but as it is very infectious and there is no known cure for it, the health authorities in France have decided to put us into quarantine. This means that you will not be allowed to catch your connections or leave the airport for the next 48 hours."

There was an angry uproar throughout the plane. And there it was, the curse! I thought I was unfortunate enough to have had sex with a man I had no idea was married and now I was stuck with him for another two days. And then I did not want to die of this swine flu thinking that he would be the last man I had been with. I looked over to Luana who seemed just as peeved. Eric was on the phone and so was Louis. My phone vibrated and I saw that I had ten unread messages.

"May I ask you to remain calm. We can't allow you off the aircraft for the moment because health authorities are preparing the quarantine room. It should be ready in the next couple of hours. Please can I ask you to kindly get back to your seats. We will update you on the situation as soon as possible. Can we also kindly ask you to place your luggage back into the overhead bins so that fellow passengers can move down the aisles. We thank you for your kind cooperation."

I put my bag back into the luggage bin and wanted to help my fifty year old neighbour who hated me do the same. He held tight onto the handle of his luggage. He gave me a courteous, but tight-lipped smile.

"Thanks. I can do it myself."

Was he afraid that I give him the swine flu or was it misplaced masculine pride? I went back to my seat. Luana was already back in hers.

"But what the hell is this thing? Have you heard about this swine flu before?" I asked Luana.

"No. Bird flu, yes, but not swine flu."

"Do you think there's a possibility we might have caught it?"

"You might have. After all, you spent the night with a pig last night."

It didn't make me laugh. I gave her a jab. Luana massaged her arm.

"What? It's true, isn't it?"

"Yes and now I'm stuck with him for two days of quarantine. The ultimate punishment for not asking whether he was married... or another consequence of Miguel's curse…"

My phone rang.

"Hello? Hi, mum. No everything's all right. We just landed, but we can't go out of the plane. Apparently, we are being quarantined for the next two days. No, we don't have much detail on how it will work. We are waiting. Me? No, I have no symptoms. Well, I don't even know what the symptoms are anyway. Tiredness? Yes, ok, but that's mainly because I didn't sleep the whole night. Coughing? No, I'm tired, but I have nothing close to a flu. Luana is fine too. She is just tired from the trip too. Yes, it was amazing. I will show you pictures when I see you. I don't know when mum, I will call you when we're out of the plane. Listen, my phone battery is almost dead. Can you tell family and friends everything's all right and I will get back to civilization in two days? Ok? Then see you soon. When I can charge my phone again, I will call you. Ok mum, see you later. Bye!"

I didn't tell my mum the whole truth and I didn't like to lie. My telephone was charged, but I didn't want her to call me every five minutes as she usually did when she was worried about me. And I didn't want to call everyone. The situation wasn't really clear and I wanted to know more before I told anything to anyone. Charlie had tried to call me three times and had texted me.

Julia, I just wanted to make sure you're ok. I saw there was an outbreak of swine flu in Mexico. Let me know when you're back.

"Charlie sent a text."

"The crazy snorer never leaves you in peace, does he?"

"No. He loves me, you know?"

"Yes, but he's completely jealous and manipulative. I don't get why you haven't got rid of him yet."

"I did, but he's still crazy about me... And let's say, it's hard to resist his sex appeal."

"It would do you good to live like a nun for some time…"

"Says the one who slept with Gabriel the whole time in Mexico?"

Eyes closed, I started thinking of Charlie, my ex whom I had left a month ago. I remembered the first time we had met.

Charlie was twenty-five years old, three years younger than me. He was still a student and lived at his parents' place. It wasn't ideal, but his lovely picture on the dating website and the funny exchanges we had had convinced me to meet him. We met in a café next to my home and when he arrived, I felt something I had never felt before.

It had nothing to do with love at first sight. It was totally animal. It was as if he used pheromones to attract me. My body felt like it was charmed, driven by lust. I didn't just want to get close to him... I had to touch him, to kiss him. To the point that it frightened me. I had had desire for men before, yes, but such an irrepressible and even uncontrollable longing for a stranger, never. I even told myself it was a dangerous reaction to have. If all the people were feeling what I was experiencing right now with a person from the opposite sex, the street would end up in an open-air orgy!

What I felt was purely sexual. Maybe it was the result of prolonged abstinence after I got dumped by the so-called love of my life. Or was it just my hormones playing a trick on me?

We had talked for half an hour, and I had somehow managed to contain my urge to get me closer to him. He had taken my hand in his, and that had caused a chain reaction. I wanted him right away. He had kissed me and it was the beginning of the end.

We had left the café in a rush, leaving a generous tip behind. I had never brought a man to my place the first night before. Even less a man I didn't know an hour ago even if I felt like I knew him from our exchanges on the Internet. With other men, I had never felt the animal lust that permeated me now. Walking the five hundred meters and up the five floors that separated us from my flat had seemed an eternity.

Charlie really had something special going on. I had admired his tanned, strong and perfectly carved body. He gave off a gorgeous smell, which made his attraction even more irresistible. He got me. Nothing existed outside of him. I had finally experienced what people call magnetism. And this didn't compare with any of my exes.

With Charlie however, there were no feelings. No, nothing like this. Just an irrepressible physical attraction. Pleasure was soon followed by regret, when he fell asleep hours later in my bed and began to snore. A snore at least as strong as his magnetism had been on me.

I wondered how the perfection of one moment could be ruined so quickly after. It was impossible to sleep. I went from paradise to hell, from a moment of ecstasy to homicidal thoughts.

If there was one thing nobody was allowed to disturb, it was my sleep. I'm a groundhog but a little nothing can wake me up. Charlie snoring next to me had the same effect as a ship entering a harbor with horns blasting every five seconds. I had tried to be patient, praying I would sleep despite the ambient noise, but that only lasted five minutes. I had tried to pinch his hand, which stopped him for about one minute before he started snoring louder–Yes it was possible! I had tried pushing him into another position. To pinch his nose too. But after an hour, nothing had worked and I was exhausted. I decided to wake him up.

"Do you know that you snore?"

"Ah... Yes, so I was told. Sorry…" he said half asleep.

"I can't sleep. Sorry to ask you this, but could you go back to your place? I really need to sleep. I had a difficult week at work and I'm exhausted. I need to catch up on some sleep."

He grabbed my alarm clock to check the time.

"Mmmh… There are no trains at this time and my parents live on the other side of Paris, in the suburbs. I'm not going back on foot."

I didn't like his answer. But I wasn't going to spend a fortune on a cab. I had to resort to plan B.

"Ok, stay there, I'm going to sleep in the living room."

"Are you sure? I can sleep there."

"No, it's ok, I'll go. The sofa-bed is a bit complicated to open. Stay here, I will take care of it."

I didn't want to sleep on this uncomfortable sofa-bed, but I had no other choice. I opened it as I could. I was too tired to make the bed. I took the blanket that usually covered the couch and wrapped myself up in it before laying on the bed.

But that didn't make much of a difference. The walls of my home–I learnt that night–, were like cardboard and I could still hear Charlie snore almost as if he was in the bed next to me. I grabbed my ear plugs even if I knew I could never bear them while sleeping. But Charlie was snoring so loudly that they were no use. After cursing him the whole night, I suddenly remembered that the first train ran about five o'clock in the morning. If Charlie could catch it, that meant that I could get some sleep, provided my neighbor didn't start drilling like he was used to on Saturday mornings. I decided to wake him up.

"Charlie?"

"Hmm? What time is it?"

"5 in the morning. I've been trying to sleep for more than three hours."

"I'm sorry, Julia."

"I know something you can do to change the situation."

He must have thought I wanted to have sex again

because he took me in his arms and started to kiss me. I gently pushed him away.

"No, I didn't mean that. At this time, trains are running so you can go home. I'm sorry to ask you this, but I absolutely need to sleep and with you snoring in the bedroom, it's impossible. Please could you leave?"

"I snore that loudly?"

"Yes."

He pulled me closer to him and started to caress me. I turned over again.

"You're sure, you don't want to?"

"Charlie, I haven't sleep all night. I'm exhausted."

"Ok, I understand. But seeing you like this, I just can't resist."

He had managed to make me forget all about that sleepless night very quickly... We had remained together three months despite his snoring. His sexual magnetism meant that I was literally stuck to him. And I had got into the habit of sending him home at night. So he never stayed over, which annoyed him, but was perfect for me.

I realised quite quickly that he wanted me for himself and that he didn't want to share me with my friends. He did everything to turn me away from them. And if a man had the misfortune to approach me, I was always afraid that it would end up in a pitched battle. Charlie was possessive and Luana had convinced me to leave him. I had tried many times, but he would always make sure we met again and every time I saw him, I would give into his magnetic trick. That's why Luana had asked me to travel with her to Mexico so I could avoid falling back into him.

I could have never fallen in love with a man who

prevented me from sleeping at night and seeing my friends during the day because he was so possessive. I decided never to use dating websites again and that I should wait for life to give me a man I truly loved. And while Charlie provided sex whenever I needed it, I wasn't so desperate to find someone.

The problem was that Charlie was madly in love with me. I told him that he would only ever be a sex friend and that must have hurt his pride. It was always the same story: you always want what you can't have. But my feelings for him never changed, on the contrary. He wanted to see me more and more often. And I just wanted to see him to have it off.

Before I left for Mexico, he had a big jealousy fit. He didn't want me to go so far away from him for two weeks. I had said that I had had enough. We couldn't go on this way. He had begged me not to leave him, that he would be content with what I had to give, even though I knew he was in pain because of this unrequited love. And I didn't want to let something go on that was not healthy for me or for him. I had left him after sleeping with him one last time. I was no fool! He was aware that this was our last time and had shown a passion on a whole new level while holding back his sadness.

He said he loved me and I was the woman of his dreams. I just wanted him to shut up to concentrate on the thing at hand. It was exactly the reason why I wanted to leave him: when a feeling is not reciprocal, it becomes unbearable. He begged me once more to stay with him, but I had made my decision.

I couldn't carry on this way. He looked totally

devastated as he left. I felt guilty to see him so low. I acted very cold, not to give him any hopes. It wasn't an easy decision because he was probably the most passionate lover I had ever had, but it was the right thing to do. One day he was bound to find a girl very soon who would appreciate him for his qualities and for his snoring…

After we broke up, I was looking forward to the trip to Mexico, to get away from Charlie and to finally have a holiday. I could only think of it.

"You're right, I can't seem to take my own advice. But you really need to stop seeing Charlie. You should try and find a good man."

"But I'm working on it, my dear Luana! With this pig I must cope with for another forty-eight hours, you will admit that I can't really put this plan into action before we get out of this bloody airport. That's, if we get out of it alive. Maybe we'll all die from this swine flu… And you will be the last person I ever held in my arms."

Luana gave me a nudge.

"Stop being such a drama queen. I don't think anyone is sick, and if someone is, surely it's because of the air con that's ten times too strong as always on planes. And if there really is a case of flu, I'm pretty sure that person will be taken straight to the hospital. Your family is super healthy and so is mine. Almost everyone is making it to their hundredth birthday on both sides. I trust our genes. You and I, we have nothing to fear. And remember what Miguel said? I'm a shaman too so if need be..."

"But I thought you didn't want tot hear about it."

"If it's to save my best friends, I'm becoming a

shaman tomorrow."

"You're a shaman already he said. Only I doubt you can start from scratch."

"When I had seen my cousin a few years ago, he had explained to me he had had to remain three days and three nights in the forest without eating, drinking or sleeping. It was his initiation. It's one of the reasons why it doesn't appeal to me so much. And also I didn't really believe in it. But given what we are experiencing, I tell myself I tell myself he must have really liked you at the time to have punished you with a curse that bad."

"I will thank your cousin my way for that, if we get out of this alive! Is there a way to do an express initiation so that I can cast spells too?"

"No idea, but I won't touch that part. I will cure you, yes. For the rest, no way."

I was disappointed. Miguel couldn't get away with it. Maybe the curse wasn't over and on top of it I would get the swine flu! Maybe I was already contaminated?

"But look at how everybody is panicking around us. I feel that everybody's afraid."

And me first and foremost! I thought.

"That's normal. They're all wondering if their neighbour is infected."

I looked at the woman next to me. She had been asleep through all of this. I really had to ask what sleeping pill brand it was. They seemed so efficient. My phone rang. It was my sister.

"Hi? How are you? No, ok. No, I don't think I'm sick and I don't see anyone with symptoms on the plane. Seriously? Fifteen days? Ok. But hold on, you're telling me that if I die, I will die alone? Thanks dear sister, it was very pleasant to speak to you one last time and to hear those words of comfort. On the contrary, I understood you very well. You don't care about me. The only thing that counts is your family. And it sounds like I am not part of it anymore. Sorry but I've got to hang up, they're making an announcement. Bye."

"Dear Passengers, we have now received more information from the airport authority. We must wait another thirty minutes before the sanitary services are ready. Each passenger will then need to be inspected by a doctor. It is likely to take time to carry out all the checks, so we ask you to bear with us and kindly remain seated until you are called. We will begin with the first row, and then in order until the last row. You can then clear customs and collect your luggage, which is waiting for you in the quarantine room. There will be toilets and showers at your disposal. You will also be provided with bed camps for the night. Two meals will be served for lunch and dinner. You will also be given bottles of water. In about forty-eight hours, you will be able to get back home or take a connecting flight. On behalf of Air Mexico, we apologise for the inconvenience caused. The crew is at your disposal to assist you. We will shortly start to call you one by one for the medical checks. We kindly ask you to keep calm and remain seated unless you need to go to the toilet. We thank you for your attention."

I glanced down at the woman next to me again. All of a sudden, I started worrying that she wouldn't wake up at all. I shook her slightly to make sure she was still alive.

"Madam?"

She wasn't answering. I shook her a little harder and

some saliva spilled out of her half-opened mouth.

"Help! Help!"

I put my hand on the top of her chest. She was still breathing. I didn't know what to do. A steward arrived. All the other passengers were hiding away in their seats for fear of being touched by my neighbour. All but me and Luana. We had already been in contact with her so if she had swine flu, then it was too late to protect ourselves against it. I helped the steward carry our neighbour to the front of the plane with Luana. Eric looked at me as if I were out of my mind, but he didn't lift a finger. A stretcher and masked firefighters in overalls soon appeared from the front door.

After she was taken out of the plane, a man in a white overall and a mask asked us to go and wash our hands. Security procedure. We complied and as we walked back to our seats, everybody watched as if we were plague-ridden. Even Louis and Eric. Luana's neighbour even got out of his seat to avoid being touched when we got back to our seats. He leant his body towards the aisle as much as he could. He even asked a steward if he could change seats. But the steward refused, the plane was full. I was thinking about my neighbour, who must have been at the hospital by that time. It was really strange. I too should have given into the panic, but I felt strangely calm.

With Luana, we had spent the next couple hours watching a movie even if it was difficult to concentrate with the permanent concert of cellphones ringing and worried conversations.

The other passengers were all panicking. I don't know if it was because my sister had just told me not to get anywhere close to her and her children in the next two weeks, but I didn't care anymore. She was afraid I had caught the swine flu. I came to realise at that very moment that I would die anyway. Whether it was today of the swine flu, or tomorrow of anything else, that didn't change much about my final destination.

I learnt a lot about human nature. For my sister, protecting her children was more important than caring about me. Thinking that my own sister could let me die alone, I realised that parental love was much stronger than sisterly love.

My mother had said nothing of the kind. On the contrary, she wanted me to come home as soon as possible to keep me away from that flu. But everyone out there - apart from her - reacted like my sister and didn't want the flu to spread to them. They had no consideration anymore for the human who carried the virus.

Suddenly, it was not only outside that everybody was suspicious of everybody else. The passengers on the plane were becoming mistrustful of their own neighbours. Everybody was trying to avoid thinking about their own death. What really mattered was to avoid catching the flu at all costs, to avoid coming in contact with other people or even breathe the same air as them. Some people had had covered their mouth constantly on their mouth and nose with their hand since the first announcement.

Luana was finally called for her medical check-up before me. Eric and Louis who were one row in front of us had already been called out too. And then it was my turn to see the doctor. Or what was left of him. Because I could only see his eyes: he was totally covered with a mask and a white overall. It was like in E.T. when the scientists come and look for Elliott and him.

He was examining me. I felt like a cow in a farm. He took my blood pressure, controlled my reflexes and my eyes. He asked me a lot of questions about where I had been in Mexico, if I had been in contact with farm or wild animals. The names of the people I had had contact with. If I knew the person I was sitting next to on the plane and if I had had any physical contact with her.

I had to tell him about my story with Eric begging him to abide by the code of medical confidentiality. The story sounded even more sordid to me now. Shagging on a plane seemed much less glamorous in those circumstances. I felt as if I was at the police station having to answer questions which I would have never wanted anyone to know about. Especially when the doctor asked if I had had a sexual intercourse. I wanted to say of course not, but my conscience told me I had to tell the truth, because if Eric had contracted the disease, I would have wanted to know. So I said yes. I didn't want to go into any details. He asked me if I was traveling alone and I told him I was with Luana. She must have been in the quarantine room already.

The doctor asked me to undress and inspected every part of my body. He didn't want to say whether my neighbour was still alive or whether she had caught the flu. I asked the only question that was important to me in my advanced state of tiredness and jet-lag.

"Is there a way we will be able to sleep in that room? I barely slept on the plane and I'm very tired."

"There will be camp-beds, which will be delivered

later. For the moment, you will have to manage with the seats in the room. Sorry."

I was disappointed. I had dreamt of a shower and a good bed. I would be on zombie mode today, like the day after my first sleepless night with Charlie.

"Ok. Can I get dressed now?"

"Yes, I have your home address and your phone. You can go to the customs."

After getting dressed I walked to the exit. The customs were immediately after. Even the police officers hidden behind their bulletproof windows were wearing a mask and white overalls. I could only see their eyes.

"Your passport, please."

I was looking frantically into my bag. The policeman made me feel nervous. My bag was full of stuff and I couldn't find my purse. Normally I would have had time to find it while I was queuing, but here I was all alone in front of the officer.

"Take your time, there's no rush."

"Thanks, I have no idea where I put it."

I must have looked for two long minutes under his scrutinizing look.

"There it is!"

He looked at the passport and the date of entry in Mexico. He entered some data on his computer and then handed the passport back to me.

I had to walk through a never ending corridor to get to the quarantine room. There was no one around. A cart with cleaning products was sitting in front of the toilets. As if the cleaner had abandoned it in haste when they heard that potentially infected people were arriving.

Freshly printed signs were indicating the direction to follow to get to the quarantine room.

I finally arrived there. Luana and I had been sitting in the middle of the plane and I wondered how the room would be able to contain the rest of the people that were still there. All the luggage of the passengers that were still on the plane was in a corner. The little staff that was there was wearing a mask and a white overall. Luana came to meet me as soon as she saw me.

"Come with me, I collected your luggage already. I found pillows and we can have a sandwich if you want."

"Well looks like you've had time to settle in while I was still in there with the doctor! I would die for a sandwich, I'm starving! But I could do with a shower before food."

"There's only three showers in the women restrooms. See if there's one free. People were queuing until now."

"I need to get a towel, some toiletries and fresh clothes out of my suitcase."

Luana pointed me to it.

"Here, I got it for you."

Luana was really a sweetheart. You could really count on her. I wasn't that surprised that she had already managed to settle in. I opened up my suitcase and started searching through my stuff. My towel started to have a musty smell: I had packed it into my suitcase as it was still wet, thinking I would wash my laundry as soon as I'd hit home. I found a dress that I had bought in Mexico. I was sure it would attract catch men's attention, and maybe Eric's. If those days were my last on Earth, then I wanted to be as pretty as can be and let him die of desire for me without ever being able to have me again. Finally I had found everything I needed and I headed for the showers. There was a free cubicle.

I opened the door. I could tell it had been used a lot already as there was wet hair all over the floor. To be honest, it was quite vile. I tried to tidy it up a bit. I quickly picked up a ball of hair with disgust and threw it in the bin outside. Then I rinsed the shower tray before I could finally start showering.

I would have eaten the sandwich before showering because I was so hungry. But the imperious need to get rid of any trace of Eric from my body was stronger. I had been smelling his odour on my skin for hours. I was still in shock after his confession and the fact that I would be stuck with him for another two days only made it worse. My only option was to ignore him completely. Or at least pretend. With everything that had happened, I had completely forgotten to ask Luana what she had told Louis, that made him blush so much. I felt tiredness suddenly take over me. I hoped it wasn't a symptom of the flu, but just weariness.

I had rubbed my skin with a vigour only equaled with the effort I put in when rubbing off grease. I had washed my hair too. I wanted to be totally rid of any trace of Eric, at least on my skin.

I dried myself and put on the dress. I wanted him to kick himself for treating me that way. I went out with my towel tied over my hair and my laundry under the arm. I looked at myself in the mirror. I had shadows under my eyes and Eric's stubble had left small red marks on my chin.

I had to remedy all this with some make up. Luckily us women could cheat from time to time. You could think I had a good night's sleep once I had my make up on.

When I walked out of the restroom, who should I find myself faced with but Eric? He looked surprised to see me and moved back a step while staring at me. He must have been afraid that I would give him the swine flu. He should have realised though that any harm had already been done. We had exchanged much more than a love note after all.

I walked away quickly, ignoring him. I didn't want to talk to him. His reaction sickened me even more. I wanted to look back, just to check if he was still watching me. But I carried on walking towards Luana, resisting the temptation to look back. It would have been a sign of weakness.

There was a lot of confusion in the luggage area. Someone was lying on the floor with people wearing white overalls and masks standing around. One of them was trying to separate a woman from the lying man, who must have been her husband. A sanitary team had arrived to take away the man on a stretcher. The woman left alone sat on a free chair and started sobbing. The people sitting next to her stood up in one go. Fear in action...

One of the men with a mask announced:

"Anyone who has been in direct contact with this man, please follow me."

I had never seen him. Immediately, the crowd had got thinner. Some people got closer to the man who had made the announcement. His wife too. I walked towards Luana.

"What happened?"

"Apparently, he has the symptoms of the swine flu."

"Did you ever notice him before?"

"Not until now."

"I'm starting to really wonder if we'll get out of this place alive."

"Don't start, Julia. I'm sure everything will be alright. Everyone is panicking but maybe this old man has nothing or something different from the flu. Like your neighbour."

"You're right. Let's not panic. Maybe we could buy a newspaper to learn more about the epidemic?"

"Nope, there's nowhere to buy one from around here."

"Too bad I only have ten pages of my book left to read. What am I going to do during the next 48 hours?"

I swept the room with my eyes to see if there was anywhere where I could charge up my phone. But they seemed all taken and I had not much battery left.

"Maybe we can ask someone to swap books?"

"Well I think for now nobody wants to touch anybody else, let alone read someone else's book. People have an irrational fear of being contaminated. Especially since we were in contact with our neighbour on the plane and nobody knows what became of her."

"You're right."

"I have a book if you want."

"I already read it."

"Really?"

"I had to do something while you were with Gabriel…"

Luana gave me a nudge.

"There's aways Eric. Now that you touched him, flu or not, it makes no difference anymore."

"If you think I'm going to go talk to him, you're crazy. By the way… What the hell did you say to Louis on the plane that made him blush that way? With all this swine flu story, I completely forgot to ask."

"Well, I'm not very proud of myself… I only said that because at the time I thought that I would never see him again."

"What was it? What did you tell him?"

"That it was a shame we hadn't used our time like Eric and you during the night. That we would have had fun."

"Are you mad?"

"I just wanted him to know that his colleague wasn't an angel. But you will notice that I chose my words wisely and didn't tip him off. I just gave him food for thought. Suggestions. I don't know what he deduced from it…"

"So that's why he can't stop looking at you?"

I had turned towards Louis and had surprised him staring at Luana. When he noticed my gaze, he had quickly turned back towards Eric. Eric was on the phone, probably with his wife. I wondered once again if he had cheated on her before me. I would probably never know.

"Hold on, does that mean Louis thinks you want to sleep with him?"

"Even if I should die tomorrow, never!"

"Never say never…"

"I could go and ask Eric if he could lend me a book… But only if he apologizes to you."

"Would you, really?"

"Yes."

"You are really so sweat. Thanks. But let's eat first,

shall we?"

"Ok, my stomach is rumbling."

Fortunately Luana had taken sandwiches for us as soon as she had arrived in the quarantine room and we also had a seat. Some people were sitting on the floor because there weren't enough chairs.

The sandwich was really dry and tasted of plastic. I drank a bit of water to make the taste go away, but it didn't help much. I was watching Eric talk on his phone from the corner of my eye. He was gesticulating. He seemed very agitated. Louis turned towards us from time to time to take a look at Luana. I pretended not to see it, but every time he would turn, I had to stop myself from laughing out loud.

I wondered what Eric had said to Louis, when he asked what had happened between us. Maybe Eric was full of remorse or maybe for him cheating was second nature and he was only figuring out how to make sure it didn't come to the ears of his wife.

I was finishing my plastic sandwich, when I saw Louis materialised next to Luana.

"Hi Luana," he said shyly.

Luana gave me a frightened look.

"Louis! So you guys from the other end of the room are not too afraid of getting close to other people?"

Luana must have been reassured that Louis hadn't asked her to sleep with him straight away.

"Yes. People are very suspicious. I feel like everybody is only thinking about survival."

I told him:

"Aren't you afraid that people will see us talking

together?"

Louis seemed surprised.

"Why?"

"Because of the lady who sat next to me on the plane…"

"She was sitting very close to us too. We breathed the same air and if she really had the swine flu, then we have probably caught it too."

Luana asked:

"Were you able to talk to your family?"

"Yes."

Louis stared at his feet and then made a big smile.

"Luana, could I talk to you in private?"

Luana looked at me frowning in a way only I could see her face and then turned her head towards him.

"Yes of course, but there is not much privacy around here."

"Maybe we could go over to that corner?"

"Ok."

When Louis set off in that direction, Luana rolled her eyes. I smiled to her and I raised my two thumbs to encourage her as she did when I went to talk to Eric in the plane. She shook her head and walked towards him dragging her feet to make me laugh. I hadn't noticed that Eric had got closer in the meantime.

"Julia, I would like to apologise."

He made me jump.

"What are you doing here?"

"I'm sorry for the things I said this morning. I didn't know what to do. It's the first time I'm unfaithful to my wife and I can't risk everything."

But of course! What a lame excuse!

"Why did you reply to my love notes then?" I asked searching for a hint of truth.

"Well... I was surprised. It's been such a long time since anyone has taken an interest in me. My life is so boring, if only you knew... Since we had our second daughter more than a year ago, my wife doesn't touch me anymore. When you wrote the notes, I didn't think anything would happen. I thought we would talk and that's it. But you were so... attractive. I couldn't resist. And now I'm lost."

Blah blah blah… Poor little abandoned husband! What does he think? That I will have pity for him?

"Look, Eric. You can say what you want, I cannot accept your apologies. You should have told me you were married. Nothing would ever have happened if I had known."

"I had planned to tell you, but you never asked and in the heat of the moment, I completely forgot."

How was it possible to forget such a thing?

"What about your ring? Why weren't you wearing it?"

"I always take it off when I'm flying. My hands get swollen. That's why I didn't have it, I swear. Everything went so fast... The situation got out of control. I just wanted you so much Julia."

"Eric, stop. Forget it. I can't accept your apologies. In two days you will go back to your wife and I will go back to my life. I never want to hear from you again."

"Julia, please, forgive me."

"No, sorry. Now go."

Eric slowly went away and then suddenly turned

around.

"I just wanted to thank you for opening my eyes to my life. Without you, I would have carried on this way instead of talking to my wife and facing our problems. I also wanted to tell you that you are really beautiful and sexy and I wish I could have resisted you. But I'm happy I didn't because I would have never touched you and that would have been a pity."

With that, he went away. Luana was still talking with Louis. I didn't know what to think. What was Eric playing at with his big declarations? He used me and threw me away. He had the nerve to ask me not to say anything to his colleague because he had a wife and children and now he wanted my absolution? Or was it the fear of dying that made him react this way? Maybe he felt remorse for his sins or maybe he was really lost and he didn't know how to react? In any case, it was all too easy and I didn't want to have anything to do with him anymore.

To my great surprise, I saw Luana lean towards Louis as if she was about to kiss him. But she just kissed him on the cheek. Then Louis walked back over to Eric with his head down while Luana headed towards me all smiles.

"So?" I asked.

"To make it short, Louis said he found me very attractive and that if I really wanted to make love before the end of the world, he was available. When I told him I only said that I wanted to sleep with him in revenge for Eric's behaviour, he got all quiet. So we talked a bit about Eric's behaviour and he said he had suggested to him to talk and apologise to you. Eric made him promise not to say anything to his wife. But Louis also told me that Eric told his wife on the phone that they needed to have a conversation. So I won an admirer and an informer. I kissed him on the cheek to console him and I told him to come with us if he was tired of Eric."

"Look at him, he looks really sad that you didn't accept his proposal."

"Poor Louis. He has no wife, no children and he's desperately looking for a girlfriend."

"And you took away all his hopes, bad girl…"

"What about Eric? What did he tell you then?"

I explained our conversation to Luana.

"Then it means that you saved him from intergalactic sexual emptiness. He didn't say anything because he perfectly knew that if you were aware he was married with two children, there was no way you would have ended up with him in the toilets of the plane. What a manipulative bastard!"

"That's exactly why I told him I didn't accept his apologies. He also confessed that he had never cheated on his wife before me. Given the liar he is, I doubt it! He also thanked me for that night and said how beautiful and sexy I was. A fat lot of good that does me! I don't know what to think of all that now."

"Nothing! This man doesn't know what he wants. Maybe it's the fear of dying that pushed him to tell you all that. Maybe he wanted to convince you to make love one last time and all that he said to you was just bullshit. I don't know. In any case, ignore him, he's not worth it."

"That's exactly what I intend to do. It's just sad that I forgot to borrow a book from him now because we won't talk anymore I think… For all I know, he must be reading something like the biography of Casanova. I'm not sure I want to read this."

"I can ask Louis if you want."

"No, I just remembered I had my MP3 player. I will listen to music, it will do me good. But now I would like to sleep. I'm tired."

"Me too…"

"A shame we don't have blankets."

"Or a bed! Maybe we can ask the guys in white overall if they have any?"

"Ok, I'll go and ask."

I knew Eric would be watching me. And I wanted him to desire me but not be able to have me. I wanted him to regret bitterly. But maybe he told himself he had reached his goal. I went to one of the masked silhouettes.

"Sorry, do you have any blankets?"

"I'm going to ask."

"I'm sitting on that side. If you can find some, could you please bring them over?"

"Yes, of course."

"Thanks."

It was frustrating to only see the eyes of a person hidden under the mask. I turned to Luana who was reading as she waited for me.

"There aren't any available apparently, but the man said that if he can find any, he will bring them to us. I'm gonna try to have a nap in the meantime."

I curled up to get to sleep, but I couldn't really find a comfortable position on these plastic seats. At least, I had more space for my legs than on the plane. Despite the jet-lag and the general exhaustion, I couldn't sleep. The air conditioning gave me goosebumps despite the jumper I had put on. I was dying for a blanket. And most of all it was impossible because I couldn't stop thinking about Eric.

The humiliation that I had felt and the shame of not having asked if he was married or if he had someone were coming back to me. It had always been obvious to me that a married man wouldn't answer to the advances made by another woman. Of course I only thought with my own system of values. It didn't come to my mind that other people could try and take advantage of me.

Now the harm had been done. And why the hell did Eric apologise now and tell me those things? I was convinced that if we hadn't found ourselves stuck in that situation, he would have disappeared from my life forever. So why come and talk to me now? Slowly fatigue took over and I let my thoughts drift away...

***

I'm on the plane. The captain announces that passengers are going to be put into quarantine for two days. Suddenly a woman of about forty years old who seems to travel alone starts shouting.

"You can't lock me in against my will! You have no right to do so! I object to being held in a room for 48 hours with people that could infect me. Let me go out right now!"

She grabs her hand luggage and walks towards the exit. On these words, a revolution breaks out on the plane. A passenger opens the doors of the plane and everybody rushes to go out. It's panic aboard… I sit still with Luana, waiting for the whirlwind to pass. But the flight attendants don't manage to contain the crowd. After all of them are gone, Luana and I go out too giving them one last commiserating look.

A queue is forming. We learn from a person in front of us, that the police is there and that they are forcing us into the quarantine room. That the woman who caused a scandal was arrested. And that we must do a medical check-up. I suddenly realise that Eric and Louis are not there and practically at the same time, I start feeling ill and I pass out.

Luana catches me before I fall. People move away from me. Only Luana is helping me and calls for help. She stares at people furiously because nobody is lifting a finger: everybody's afraid to touch me. Luana gets me back on my feet somehow. I come to my senses and I start walking with the little strength that I have left. Luana puts my arm around her shoulder. Everybody keeps their distance even if they see how we struggle to walk side by side in the narrow corridor. People move away and are terrified my clothes might brush them. We arrive at the doctor's office. He opens the door and sees the state I am in.

"Hold on a minute please," he says.

He shuts the door. Luana is exhausted and I feel that this long wait is discouraging her completely. This doctor should be helping us not having us waiting. He opens the door again after a minute that seemed like an eternity to us. With him are two men with a stretcher in overalls and masks. They lay me down on it and I feel worse. A sharp pain goes through my body and I can't move anymore. I see Luana staring at me in distress. I can't talk anymore to reassure her. Nothing comes out of my mouth. I pass out. It's a black hole. I wake up in the hospital. I try to get up, but I have no strength to do it. Luana moves closer to me.

"Don't move!" she says.

"Where are we?"

"At the hospital."

"Do I have the swine flu?"

"They think so, yes."

"What about you?"

"We don't know. They didn't want me to stay with you, but I told them that I would never leave you alone. If anything happens, we're a team. You're my best friend, Julia. They put me under observation with you because you have all the symptoms of a normal flu. Maybe it's only the flu. I don't know any more than that at this stage."

"What about Eric and Louis? Are they in the hospital too?"

"No idea… I can't get out of the room. They locked us in. They all carry masks to protect themselves from us."

She caresses my hair.

"It would be ridiculous to die here."

I fall asleep. In my dream I see Miguel. He's surrounded by a jaguar and a bear. He utters words I don't understand and seem to inhale through his mouth something in my body that he spits out.

***

I suddenly woke up. I was still sitting in the quarantine room. Except for the pain in the neck and shoulders from sitting in that uncomfortable position I didn't feel anything from the exhaustion I felt in my dream. I looked around me. Luana was sleeping. It was 3:27pm. I couldn't resist looking in Eric's direction. He looked at me and smiled.

I pretended I didn't notice and went to the toilets. A woman opened the door in front of me using a strip of toilet paper, probably to protect herself from the bacteria on the door handle. But what could she protect herself from? The virus was in the air and a strip of toilet paper was not going to keep the swine flu away. If she wanted to protect herself, it was too late.

It would have been a pity to die now, indeed. I would never have known the joy of being a mother. I would never have been a married woman. But I had seen many things. At least more than a dying baby. I was thinking about what Eric said. I started to understand why he said those things to me.

Now that the shadow of death was hovering above our heads, it was not a time to lie or pretend anymore. It was now or never that one should live as if there was no tomorrow. Because maybe there wasn't going to be one. Maybe I would end up in the hospital with Luana as in my dream spending my last two days on earth suffering terribly. I didn't know if Miguel could heal remotely and if his type of medicine could cure me. In my dream, that was my impression. As if he had taken away the virus from my body.

Now everything had changed. I could decide to give

Eric a second chance. I could spend my last 48 hours in his arms and get a little tenderness in a world where everybody was afraid of brushing past someone else. I could decide to go and talk to him or rather take advantage of him too. Wasn't he the best lover I ever had? And now that the curse was lifted, I might as well make the most of him if I had to die. I finished brushing my teeth and got back next to Luana who was still asleep. I took her hand.

"Luana. I need to talk to you."

She widened her eyes. She must have been wondering why there was such an urgent tone in my voice.

"Hmm. I'm listening…"

"If we must all die here, then I should forgive Eric and spend my last moments in his arms. At least I would feel loved. And this illusion is the only thing I need right now."

Luana took me in her arms and held me tight:

"And now, don't you feel loved?"

"Of course, I do, but you know what I mean."

"Yes, I do."

"So then, you would be ready to forgive everything that happened because you realised you could die tomorrow?"

"Exactly."

"Julia, sorry to say it this way, but we will all die eventually… Tomorrow or any other day. We could have died in a car crash in Mexico or in a plane crash… Is this really the first time you consider things from this angle? Because it's true of your entire life actually… I don't think that throwing yourself into the arms of a man who behaved like a pig is the solution."

"But he tried to apologise."

"What if we all survive?"

"I'm not in love with him. I don't plan on seeing him after this. He'll go back to his family and I'll go back to looking for the man of my dreams. I don't have a book to read, so I might as well do something constructive and reconcile with the human kind. Maybe I will discover that I can really forgive him? I just realised that life is much shorter than I thought. Until now, I'd never thought I could die any minute from an unknown disease."

"You're right. Maybe I should give Louis a chance too."

"Are you serious?"

"Of course not! I was kidding. He's very nice, but I prefer to die alone. Come on, admit that Eric is the best sex you ever had and that's the reason why you want to make up."

"I admit that this prospect would help me a lot if I must forgive him, that's right…"

"Naughty girl! We can kill time with them if you wish…"

"Ok, but I must talk to Eric in private first."

"Ok. I'll wait for you here."

I went straight to Eric. He watched me with curiosity and his smile got larger as I approached.

"Eric, can I talk to you for a minute?" I asked.

"Yes, of course."

"Come with me."

I took him to a corner where there was no one about. I took my courage in both hands.

"Eric, I thought about our situation and what you told me and I decided to forgive you."

He seemed surprised.

"What do you mean, forgive me?"

"If we must all die in the coming days, then I don't want to go with any hard feelings towards you. It doesn't mean I agree with what you did. You were a real bastard not to tell me the truth from the start, and to run away once your little secret was out. And you hurt me because I felt used."

"I'm so sorry. Forgive me. As I told you I was overwhelmed by the events."

"I forgive you. What is done is done. Let's move on. I think that now that Louis knows about us and Luana too, we might as well spend time together. It would be smarter than staying each in our corner waiting to see if we're all going to die. What do you think of that?"

"Of course, come with Luana. Louis will be happy to talk with her."

"OK, but I'd rather you came over to our side."

"Why not? We will take our stuff and come."

"I just want to say the truce is for forty-eight hours only. After that, we will never see each other again. You go back to your life and I go back to mine. But at least we will have lived what might be our last days without hate."

"Fine by me."

He took my hand in his and lay a kiss on it.

"Thank you."

I wanted to go back to our seats but he held me.

"What made you change your mind?"

"I dreamt I was going to die from this disease. It

seemed extremely real. And that made me realize I didn't want to leave from this earth with any disputes or regrets. And then…"

I hesitated to tell him.

"Let's say I'd rather go to seventh heaven before going six feet under."

He laughed.

"Do I owe my redemption to my mile high prowesses."

"Possibly..."

He let go of my hand to go towards Louis. I felt strangely relieved. I still was mad at him for not telling me he had a family. But I had decided to live as if that day was the last and to believe his version.

I realised that our neighbours got frightened when they saw two men walking over to our corner. I was getting tired of this kind of reaction, but I knew this was down to the survival instinct.

"You don't happen to have playing cards by any chance?" I asked.

"No, but Louis knows many jokes…" said Eric turning towards him.

Louis spent the whole afternoon telling them. We were probably the only ones laughing in the room. Louis knew a ton of jokes and once he started, he couldn't be stopped. Even our neighbours seemed to be softening up, and were smiling and sometimes even laughing.

It was a beautiful moment in a dark atmosphere. It almost made me forget we were quarantined at the airport. From time to time I looked at Eric and he winked at me. Like an invitation to come into his arms. I was still burnt by his lie and I realised it would be hard to really forgive him totally. I was still mad at him somehow. But I knew this feeling wouldn't change anything. I had never cheated on anyone but I couldn't be sure that it would never happen to me.

If my partner refused me sex for a year, would I have cheated on him too? I was not quite sure about it. And that is what helped me to forgive him. That and the imminence of my own death made me realise that it wasn't worth bearing grudges against anyone. I understood better the meaning of *going in peace*. Because in the end not forgiving others is not forgiving oneself. I was annoyed at myself for not asking him about his relationship status. Forgiving him, was also forgiving myself for transgressing my own values.

I couldn't help thinking about the curse Luana's cousin put on me. If I had always doubted the incredible consequences that he predicted, now there was no doubt allowed. Miguel really was a great shaman, just like his father.

It was 7pm and I was getting hungry. I supposed everybody else was too. Even more because there was nothing else to do but wait and eat. I hoped there would be something hot and not a dry sandwich like the one we had earlier.

When the food arrived, it was as if a sleeping city had suddenly awoken. Everybody stood up in a minute, ready to fight to get a bite. It was incredible to see how in this situation, primal needs were showing so obviously. Like everyone else Luana and I joined the forming queue. Eric was behind me. Everybody carefully avoided to come into contact with their neighbours, which was all the more curious since everybody was rushing to get food. The result was an odd crowd, which wanted to move forward while keeping its distance.

Suddenly I felt Eric's arms around me. I didn't expect it at all, but I gave into the warmth of his arms, the comfort of being held facing this uncertain destiny. For this and the small kisses he trailed in my neck I felt I was right to forgive him, I knew it now. But I didn't want Luana or Louis to be the third wheel. I whispered in his ear:

"Listen Eric, you can hold me in your arms, but don't kiss me, I don't want Luana and Louis to feel uneasy because of us."

"Ok. But that's not going to be easy to resist you…"

I did everything I could to concentrate on our conversation with Luana and Louis while Eric was holding me in his arms, but it was impossible. I felt like each centimeter of my body in contact with his was sending me in another dimension. I felt his breath on my neck and I couldn't think of anything else. In the end I asked him to hold my hand instead, because having him so close to me was just having too much of an effect on me.

He didn't seem very pleased about it, but he agreed and took my hand instead. That was only a tiny improvement because my entire attention was now focused on the skin of his hand against mine. It was our turn at last. The food was wrapped in a bag. There was a tomato, a cheese sandwich that time–Hallelujah–a banana and a bottle of water. I made a half-turn to get back to my seat.

The man I had asked for blankets earlier was walking towards me.

"In a few minutes, we're going to distribute the bed-camps and blankets but because you asked for some first, here are two."

"Thank you so much!"

After that, he announced that people should queue next to the food counter so that the foldable beds and blankets could be distributed too.

People were fighting to get into the queue while trying to stay at a distance of each other. It was like a ballet of fear. The choreography was simple: move forward but avoid your neighbour. The men in white overalls and masks kept saying there would be one for everyone. But the survival instinct was too strong. I could see it everywhere and until this day, I had never understood its significance. Everybody was just thinking about surviving, about not being infected by their neighbours, while I was only thinking about Eric's arms. Life was a question of priorities…

Suddenly I heard cries on the other side of the room. A person was on the ground and people had stepped aside instinctively instead of trying to help. A man in a mask had arrived right away. He checked the person's pulse and put an emergency blanket over them. I couldn't see if it was a woman or a man. Other men in overalls arrived with a stretcher and the person was transported outside of the room. Nobody had raised a finger. Everybody had seen that person fall without helping them. I felt like throwing up.

It reminded me of my sister's reaction who had asked

me not to get close to her and her family for two weeks. She was prepared to leave me to die alone. I could see that exact same reaction in the eyes of the others. That further convinced me that I had made the right decision about Eric. Even if it was only the illusion of the moment, knowing I wasn't alone to confront all of this reassured me. Louis turned around:

"Did you see what just happened?"

"Yes and at this rate, we will all be dropping like flies by tomorrow, I said."

"Tomorrow or the day after tomorrow, it doesn't make any difference anymore…" commented Luana.

We spent the rest of the evening talking about everything and nothing, but also about the situation and the fear of dying. About the disease. People had unfolded their beds and I was surprised people could still circulate around them now after they were all spread out. Everywhere people were trying to sleep. There was nothing else to do anyway... Between the ones who coughed, those who snored, those who were conversing in hushed voices and the lights on, sleeping was a challenge... And I didn't even mention the planes which were taking off and landing all the time.

I was exhausted, but the presence of Eric, Luana and Louis kept me awake. Around 9.30pm, we decided it was time to sleep. My bed was unfolded next to Eric's. I kissed him for a long time before we fell asleep. We couldn't sleep in each other's arms as each bed could only fit one. I realised I was much more attracted to him than I wanted to admit. He was wearing a close-fitting t-shirt that highlighted his muscular arms that I would have wanted to touch. But I was too tired. I managed to fall asleep despite the surrounding noise.

***

Miguel sits cross-legged across from me in the tall grass. There is a little ball of energy above his head. He closes his eyes while it enters through the top of his head into his body. When he opens them, he starts dancing as if he were an animal. Then the ball of energy gets out of his mouth and goes inside of me the same way. It transforms me into a cheetah. I feel strangely calm. I can hear its words in my head:

"Don't be afraid, you are protected. The curse is over. Nothing can happen to you."

***

I woke up with the burning kisses of Eric. I kept my eyes closed savouring the taste of his mouth. I whispered:
"What time is it?"
"It doesn't matter…"
Everybody was asleep. He suddenly lifted me out of the bed and I had to hold back a little cry of surprise. It gave me the same feeling in the stomach as on a roller coaster because he had lifted me so quickly. He was squeezing me tight against him and began to zigzag across the room. Where was he taking me? He put me down in front of the toilets. I laughed.
"There seems to be a theme here."

"Open the door."

There was no one about. No noise. He walked to a door I hadn't noticed: the toilets for disabled people. I looked at him without understanding.

"But if someone wants to get in?"

"Did you see anyone in a wheelchair in the room? Get in quickly before we get noticed."

I went inside the toilet, which was much bigger than the ones on the plane. Much bigger…

"You're trying to demonstrate that our story is stuck in the toilets, is that it?"

"For the moment, I'm afraid yes."

"What about your wife? Sorry to bring up the subject, but my conscience is not totally ok with the fact that I'm stealing you from her."

"Julia, you made me understand that things are totally going pear-shaped between my wife and me since the birth of our daughter. I don't know what the future holds, maybe I will leave her, maybe this situation is the shock that I needed to put our relationship back on track, or maybe I will never want to leave you."

"We both know that the latter isn't an option."

"But you don't know how our feelings will evolve. We don't know nothing at the moment."

"Eric, there can't be a future between us. After these 48 hours, you will go back to your life and I will go back to mine. That was the deal."

"Yes, I know. You're right. Then let's make love as if we were going to die tomorrow. Without any guilt."

He kissed me intensely, as if it was really the last time.

"I've been wanting to kiss you all day long."

"I know, I put on this dress to make you feel bad for treating me like this. It seems to have worked."

"You're diabolical!"

"Let's not reverse roles here."

Eric pulled me to him laughing and squeezed me against him before kissing me passionately like the day before. He took my dress off in a flash and removed my underwear as he kissed me. I started undressing him too. He closed the lid of the toilet seat and sat me down. Then he kneeled. My body was entirely at his mercy. His fingers were giving me such pleasure. I didn't even know it was possible to come as many times in a row. In the end I begged him to stop and started to kiss him before asking:

"Do you have a condom?"

We may be dying, yes, but my preservation instinct was telling me that if it wasn't going to be the case, it was better not to get pregnant or top it up with an S.T.D.

"Yes. Just so you know, it's the last one."

"I have a dozen in my bag."

He laughed.

"Good planning, my dear."

"Well I am single, sir!"

A veil of sadness covered his eyes.

"Sorry, I didn't mean to... We said forty-eight hours without thinking about all that."

I took the lead. I squeezed his body against mine as if it was the last time we were going to have sex. And who knows, it may well be the case. I was caressing his back and started accelerating the movement. I kept kissing him all the while. I had never felt such a passion. Death was looming, but the survival instinct was there, always stronger. Eros and Thanatos. This time, he was the one who had to bite his fist when it was his time to come...

***

We had come back to our beds. Luana and Louis were sleeping peacefully. I took a look at the clock on the wall. It was 5 a.m. I couldn't believe it was that late...or early depending on how you viewed it. I was wondering when Eric had woken me up. I yawned and laid down. I heard Eric put his bed closer to mine. He then took my hand in his. I closed my eyes and kissed his hand gently. He kissed mine. If I did not wake up, at least I would have lived these last, intense moments. I was so exhausted that I fell asleep immediately.

CHAPTER 5
THE DAY AFTER

I was woken up by a crying baby. It was 6.30 in the morning. How I wished it would stop immediately so that I could get back to sleep. I blocked my ears, then tried to pull the blanket over my head but nothing worked. I remembered that they had given us earplugs on the plane. I started to look agitatedly into my bag and found them. Eric opened one eye while I was putting them on. He seemed exhausted, at least as much as I did. He whispered:

"Do you have some for me?"

"No, sorry. They handed them out on the plane, didn't you get any?"

"Yes maybe, but I didn't keep them."

"I hope the baby will stop crying soon."

I looked around me. The mother had gone to the toilets with the child. There was less noise now. I tried to get back to sleep. But I woke up again, because a ray of light had chosen to land in the middle of my face. I turned to the other side, but there was light everywhere.

A beautiful sunny day was beginning outside and it didn't seem like we were going to take advantage of it. I put the blanket over my head, but it didn't make much difference. I was now fully awake. Eric and Louis were still asleep, but Luana was no longer in her bed. I looked around to see if she was sitting anywhere, but I couldn't see her. In a panic, I went straight to the toilets to check she was there. She was putting her make up on. She had already had a shower apparently, her hair was still wet. She saw my reflection in the mirror.

"Hello Julia!"

"When I didn't see you in your bed, I thought about the worst…"

"Well, you see, I'm not dead yet. You seem totally exhausted though."

"I'll sleep when I'm dead."

Given the situation, my joke didn't make Luana laugh.

"I'm kidding, don't make that face! I'll be right back."

I went to the toilets. There were not too many people at that time. Maybe it was also because the baby was still screaming. Two toilets were busy and I didn't really want to talk about my night to Luana with people eavesdropping on our conversation. But the quarantine room wasn't exactly the ideal place either. I went out of the toilets. Luana was waiting for me.

"Come with me."

I opened a door and pulled her into the toilet for disabled people where I had spent the night with Eric. I shut the door.

"What are you doing?"

"I don't want anyone to interrupt us or listen in."

The place seemed very different from last night. I had a hard time thinking what had happened a few hours ago. Everything seemed so surreal. Maybe I dreamt it? No, I could still smell Eric's odour on me.

"That's where we hid last night."

"But it's all wet everywhere. Was it so dirty that you had to clean up everything afterwards?"

I elbowed her.

"Ouch!"

"No, we just had a shower."

"Together?"

"Yes."

"Tell me you used protection!"

"Yes, of course, you know me."

"Then the end of the world won't happen, because if you used a condom, it means you have the hope to survive this forced quarantine…"

"You don't think we will survive?"

"Of course, I do…"

"What I concluded from the last twenty-four hours is that there's nothing more important than living the present moment. There's always hope. It would be really stupid to get pregnant or catch AIDS if I am to live to a hundred years old and that flu has no effect on me. Especially if he already has two children, a wife and that he doesn't live in the same city as me."

"I agree. I also think if we are to survive this it is better not to take risks. Shall we go back to our seats?"

In the room there was a big uproar. A good part of the beds had been folded and gathered in a corner of the room. Everybody was awake and busy gathering their stuff. As if we were about to leave this place, even though we were supposed to stay another twenty-four hours... Eric was sitting on his bed and was talking on the phone. I could only see his back. He didn't see me come and I decided to keep my distance to listen in on him. I admit it, it was pretty bad of me. But I can't help it, I'm curious. From his tone, I could feel that his wife was on the other end.

"But you can't stop me seeing the girls and stay out of the way for two weeks! Where do you expect me to go? To my mum's? No but can you hear yourself? Stay in a hotel? Are you completely out of your mind Stella? What nonsense are they talking about on TV, for Christ's sake? I am perfectly fine! Ok, you want me to stay away for two weeks and send you a letter after that which proves I did all the tests? And do you want the divorce letter with it too? No? Stella, do you realise what you're asking me to do? That's it, let the media do their job and make you paranoid. You don't care where I'm going? And if I die, will you come and leave flowers on my grave or will you be too afraid of catching the flu? I'm thanking you for being such a compassionate human being. Bye!"

Eric turned off his phone. Louis who was standing in front of me looked at Eric intensely and made a gesture to tell him that I was behind him. He turned around and went to me.

"Sorry Julia, it was my wife."

"So I heard."

Our deal couldn't work. He was married and even though I tried to ignore it, it was a very real fact. I wish I could have gone out. I could only go into the bathroom. I felt like going there at that moment and turned but he retained my wrist.

"No, don't go away. Come here, I'm going to explain."

He took me in his arms and whispered in my ears:

"She reacted like your sister. She thinks I can contaminate the whole family. She doesn't want me to get close to the children during two weeks. She wants me to send her the results of the blood tests before I come back. They have all gone crazy outside, believe me!"

"So what are you going to do?"

"I don't know. Louis talked to our company and they don't want us back in the office for the next two weeks. So I am on holiday, but I can't go home. They're all afraid. The media say we're all contagious and dangerous. That they should block us in this airport for two weeks without letting anyone go so the epidemic can be contained. Apparently those who were allowed out and taken to hospital are under high surveillance. Two of them are dead."

"My plane neighbour?"

"I don't know. I didn't have time to ask. But there are other planes coming from Mexico and while you were in the toilet, they said they were letting us out to allow space to the flight coming today. The airport hasn't the capacity to keep all passengers in quarantine for more than a day."

"But that's great. That means we can go home!"

"You can, yes. I can't."

"Isn't destiny just crazy? Yesterday morning I hated you and I thought I would never see you again after we got out of the airport. And this morning when I woke up, I was a bit sad that we only had twenty-four more hours to enjoy together. And now you're telling me your wife won't let you go home?"

I thought hard. The idea of having a sex god at home for another few days didn't sound that terrible. His wife's loss was my gain and never mind the morals.

"Ok, if you want, you can come and stay at my place. Nobody's expecting me... How you will explain this to your wife, I have no idea, but you're welcome to stay... Maybe we'll die, maybe we'll survive, but at least we will have experienced something unique. After that, we'll go back to our old lives and won't ever see each other again. So what do you say? Shall we extend our pact? Do you want to spend the next two weeks on holiday with me in Paris or do you want to stay with Louis in Bordeaux in a hotel until your wife lets you come home?"

"Are you sure, Julia?"

"Yes, perfectly sure."

"Then I accept."

I whispered in his ear:

"At last we will be able to get to the "bed" stage."

He laughed and kissed me.

"You're really special, Julia. I will never forget it. And now we should prepare and get in the queue because everybody needs to be examined again before they can get out. It's already very long, look…"

I turned around and saw a group of people waiting. They were using their luggage as a shield to protect themselves from others. I turned towards Luana.

"Luana, I can't wait to get away from here. I'm going to queue for us four. When you're done with your luggage, you can join me. And then you can keep my place in the queue while I'm packing up my stuff? Deal?"

"Ok, deal."

"Eric and Louis, I'm queuing for you guys too."

I couldn't believe this strange twist of fate. The

situation was surreal. I was about to spend two weeks with a married man far away from the world, without any obligation to work (or at least I hoped my work would give me time off too) without anything to do but make love all day, sleep and eat. People in the queue around me looked as afraid as they had been since the beginning. They kept themselves a meter away from me. I had almost forgotten about this climate of fear in Eric's arms and I secretly thanked him for being with me last night and allow me to put into perspective the whole situation.

I vaguely remembered about the bird flu in China and people who were wearing masks on the streets. But panic hadn't seem to have spread as frantically then as it had here in the last twenty-four hours. I felt like the world had gone completely mad. This flu had changed my life in a way I couldn't have imagined twenty-four hours ago. It was strange to see human madness from close up.

After an hour's wait, the doctor examined me and gave me a protection mask. The TV cameras were waiting for us outside to interview the "Mexican" travelers, ready to turn the most insignificant detail of a story into a sensational piece of news, which would loop on screen. Maybe they expected us to faint live on TV. That would have made for a great scoop.

We had been surrounded by people in overalls and masks, so it felt unreal to see people dressed normally outside. We were the only ones to wear masks. I didn't want to be interviewed: given the general panic caused by this epidemic, I didn't want to be stigmatized by all the people from France. Furthermore I didn't have time to put make up on…

Louis had to arrange a connecting flight. We had said our goodbyes and it had taken Louis a little more time to leave Luana. But I could understand it, after I had seen men revolve around Luana during my whole life.

Luana, Eric and I had taken a cab with our masks on. When the taxi driver had asked us where we came from, we lied and said: « From England. » so as not to raise suspicion. He had asked why we were wearing masks and we had to explain that we were all given one at the airport. He said he was afraid to take a passenger from Mexico in case he might catch the swine flu so he wore a mask too. We pretended we were very scared too. We dropped Luana off at her place, promising we would call each other every day to check in on our respective health status and then we arrived at my place.

CHAPTER 6
PARIS

I wasn't sure anymore in which state I had left my flat so I asked Eric to stay on the landing for a quick check. I froze when I saw my ex Charlie in front of my door!

As soon as he saw me, he literally threw himself at me and took me in his arms. I was so shocked I let him do. Then he tried to kiss me and that's when Eric coughed to signal his presence. He can't have understood anything what was going on as I hadn't told him anything about my invasive and sickly jealous ex. I extracted myself from Charlie's embrace.

"What are you doing here?"

"Julia, I was scared to death. You didn't reply to my messages and my calls so I thought something had happened… When the news on TV said that you were finally out of the airport, I came straight to meet you."

He stared at Eric.

"Who's that?"

"That's Eric. Eric, meet Charlie.

Eric held his hand to shake Charlie's. Charlie gave him a floppy hand-shake.

"Nice to meet you," Eric said.

"Charlie and I broke up a month ago, didn't we Charlie?" I asked.

Charlie looked at me visibly upset that I got things straight so obviously.

"Who are you?" Charlie asked to Eric.

I didn't let Eric answer, as I was better experienced at controlling the oddity.

"I met Eric on the plane, he had nowhere to go so I asked him to come here for two weeks until he can go back home with his family. As a matter of fact, you shouldn't be here and you shouldn't be holding me in your arms. Imagine if I had the swine flu?"

Charlie didn't seem satisfied with my answer.

"Julia, whatever, I'd rather die than be separated from you any longer. You have no idea the hell I have been through waiting for your return especially after the news broke that there was a swine flu epidemic. Can I talk to you alone for a second?"

Oh no, I had always feared never ending conversations with him.

"Yes, of course. Eric, do you mind waiting for us outside for a bit? I will come and get you when we're finished."

"Do you know where I can buy a paper in your neighbourhood? I'd like to catch up on the latest updates."

I indicated to him where to find the closest newsstand. He ventured before leaving:

"Ok, are you sure you're going to be alright?"

"Yes, don't worry."

I was hoping he wouldn't feel the hint of anguish in my voice. Eric went down the stairs with a last glance. I saw Charlie tighten up. As soon as my door was closed, Charlie grasped my arm violently.

"And now will you explain to me who that guy is?"

"Let go of me, you're hurting me!"

He quickly loosened his grip as if he was surprised by the strength with which he had reacted.

"I'm sorry, I didn't mean to hurt you. So you slept with him, didn't you?"

I didn't want to answer his question head on, but he didn't leave me with a choice.

"Look Charlie, it doesn't matter. We are no longer a couple, I do whatever I want now."

Charlie stared at me looking puzzled.

"Have you forgotten about me already?" he said plaintively.

"No, I haven't forgotten about you. I will never forget you. But I've already told you I'm not in love with you. That's why I broke up with you."

I had the impression I had to explain the same thing over and over again to a child who didn't want to understand or worse still, who pretended he didn't understand. The worst was that we already had had this conversation a hundred times before our definitive break up.

"I was hoping when you got back..."

Damn his magnetic power. It was still there. It was clear I should never see Charlie again. His presence had awoken the animal in me. He had to go or I was going to lose control soon.

"Charlie, it's not the right time to talk and you shouldn't be here. Both Eric and I were on the plane and who knows we might have caught the swine flu. You should go. I would never forgive myself if you caught it by my fault. Come, wash your hands before you leave and don't touch me again."

"Never touch you again? But Julia, I'm crazy about you. If you have the flu, then I want to die with you. In the last month, I understood I couldn't live without you. I need you so much, Julia. I came to propose…"

He put his knee on the ground and took a box out of his pocket. I couldn't believe what I was seeing.

"Julia, do you want to marry me?" he said showing a ring.

I had been ignoring all of his messages, his phone calls and his emails for the past month. And I thought I had managed to get rid of him. I had been so wrong!

"But Charlie, I already told you this is over. We won't get back together. I haven't changed my mind."

"It's because of Eric, isn't it?"

I hoped Eric would take time to read the papers on a bench because it would take some time.

"No, Eric has nothing to do with a decision I took a month ago, well before I met him, remember?"

I had to be more frontal so that he goes away at last.

"I'm not in love with you Charlie. I never loved you and I can't stay with you if I haven't got feelings for you. It wouldn't be fair on you. You deserve a woman who loves you completely and I'm not the one. I could pretend, but there would be a day when I would fall in love with someone else and I would leave you. It's better that end this forever. You know it too. I left you a month ago!"

"But Julia, it's been hell being away from you. When I saw your life was in danger, I thought I was going mad. I'm begging you Julia, I need you."

He got closer to take me in his arms, but I pushed him away. For sure, Charlie was a leech that was difficult to get rid of.

"No. Sorry, but it's impossible."

He tried to take me in his arms again. I sighed.

"I know right now you want to make love to me," he said. You always told me that you couldn't resist me. That I was your best lover. How can I have that effect on you and yet I can't seem to make you fall in love with me?"

Did I ever say that to him? If I had known he would hang onto that to try and make me come back, I would have kept it for myself.

"Look," I said, "I can't explain it to myself. I don't feel anything else than a physical and sexual attraction to you."

"But how is it possible Julia?"

I was exasperated. It felt like we were going through our break-up all over again, a month later. It had taken me three hours at the time to get rid of him.

"Charlie, do you really want us to go through it all over again? Nothing has changed in a month you know. I didn't wake up all of a sudden thinking I was totally in love with you. And I'm no longer free."

It scared me to see Charlie's face twitching.

"I knew it! I'm going to smash that bastard's head."

And before I could even react, he had opened the front door of the apartment. Eric was in the doorway, ready to ring my bell. Charlie jumped on him.

"You son of a bitch!" he yelled.

Eric took a step back, which didn't prevent Charlie from giving him a blow so strong that Eric ended up on the floor. I screamed.

"Are you out of your mind? Leave him alone. He has nothing to do with it."

Charlie wasn't listening to me anymore, he leapt forward to strike Eric again. This time, he readied his foot to kick into Eric's ribs. I had no other choice but to jump onto Charlie's back to stop him.

"Let go of me!" he yelled. "It's between me and him."

I hung onto him with all my strength to prevent him from hitting Eric again, who was still stunned and was trying to get back on his feet.

"Listen to me!" I said. "It's between you and me. If you must fight against someone, fight against me."

"I will never lay a hand on you my love. But I'm going to slay him."

But what a mule head! He managed to free himself from me away. I clutched his legs to stop him punching Eric.

"Stop or I call the police!" I yelled.

Eric had managed to get up. His nose was bleeding. I was keeping the pressure on Charlie's legs.

"Run Eric and call the police. He won't do anything to me."

I saw Eric hesitate, but when he saw my insisting look, he ran down the stairs. Charlie was struggling to free himself.

"Let go of me Julia!"

He gave me a kick in the shoulder.

"Ouch!"

I started to weep from the pain. Charlie became gentle as a lamb again.

"Julia, did I hurt you?"

"No, Charlie, I'm just pretending!"

Well, visibly it wasn't time to make sarcasms... Charlie took me in his arms and got his lips close to mine. For a bit I would have given him a slap like for Miguel, but seeing where it had led me, I changed my mind. I pushed him away suddenly, furious.

"Leave me alone. You did enough harm for today. Go now! I never want to see you again here."

"But Julia, you are the woman of my life. We're going to get married you and me, you'll see…"

"Charlie, it's over now, can you hear me? Over! There's no you and me and I will never be your wife. You can bring back the ring to where you took it from."

Charlie stared at me, visibly saddened.

"Can you swear you don't want me?"

"Yes, I can swear it. I can't bear violent men."

It was true.

"Go. Now!" I ordered.

"I need you, Julia."

But when would he at last go away?

"I don't."

"Please."

He knelt down and put his arms around me. This guy was not only a leech, he was now also officially a cannonball at my feet!

"For the last time, go! I don't want to see you ever again!"

"But I can't live without you…"

What to do? How can you reason someone who can't let go?

"Nonsense! You just proved it this past month."

"But it was hell without you."

He always had a parade for each argument. I was exasperated.

"Charlie. Stop! This is never going to work. You have to find someone else."

I didn't want to tell him how his terrible snoring was getting on my nerves and the way he always wanted to be with me, as if he had no life of his own. I didn't want to have a little dog following me all the time, but a man with his own interests and hobbies. And who didn't want to spend all his spare time with me systematically.

"Charlie. You will always have a special place in my heart, but you know we are not meant for each other."

"What about him? Is he?"

"It's more complicated than you think. Eric gets back to Bordeaux in two weeks and I will never see him again after that."

"So you are playing with the both of us?"

"I don't play, Charlie. Now go and only call me if you think you caught the swine flu. You took a huge risk coming here."

"I don't care if I die. If I'm not with you, life isn't worth living."

If he wanted to take me by the feelings, it didn't work.

"Charlie, I can't let you say such a thing. There are so many women who would dream to be with you."

"All but the one I want."

Damn. Deal with it!

"I'm sure the woman of your life will come soon."

"You're the woman of my life, Julia."

I was beyond exasperation. This conversation had to end or I would soon go crazy.

"Charlie, the woman of your life wouldn't want to leave you. I'm not her. And now, I'm asking you for the last time to leave."

He pulled me to him.

"I love you, Julia."

I couldn't respond anything similar.

"I know, Charlie. But now it's really the end."

He started crying in my arms. I was not going to hug or kiss him. I didn't want to encourage him. I was standing there like a dead weight.

"Charlie. We can't stay this way. It's time for you to go."

"I want to stay here, against you."

"It's not possible, Charlie. Please."

After what felt like an eternity, he let me go. My coldness got the better of him. He looked at me with his eyes full of tears. I was wondering what the hell Eric was doing in the meantime. Maybe he had got scared and had taken a train to Bordeaux. Had he called the police like I asked?

I took Charlie's hand and walked him to the door that I opened waving goodbye at him. He did not move.

"Goodbye, Charlie."

"But…"

"Goodbye."

He looked down to the floor and finally passed the threshold. He gave me a last look like a beaten dog.

"Goodbye," he asnwered.

"Farewell."

I didn't leave him enough time to respond and closed the door. I hoped he wouldn't try to ring again. I opened the peephole to see if he was going away. He had his eyes on the floor. After a minute, I saw him go down the stairs. I went to the window to check he had left the building. Then I rushed to my phone to call Eric.

He had gone to A&E where he was still waiting to be seen by a doctor. He had called the police. They had asked him to come and file a claim, but that they wouldn't come to the scene. They were calling him now so we hung up.

It gave me time to clean up the mess, get rid of the blood stains and to congratulate myself for resisting Charlie. I went out to buy some groceries as I waited for Eric to call back. When I came home, still no call. I tried to phone him again but he didn't pick up.

I started to prepare something to eat for both of us to eat because I was getting hungry. Maybe he was getting stitched up. Besides at the emergencies, you always wait for hours... I started to eat and tried to call him. Still no one on the other end. I left a message saying to call when he would get out.

I lay down on the bed and helped by my digestion and tiredness it didn't take me long to fall asleep. Four hours later I woke up with a start. The phone was blasting its ringtone: I had left the volume to the maximum and the mobile phone right next to my hear. A deep voice said:

"Is this Julia Fletcher?"

"Yes, who are you?"

"I'm a police officer in your borough. I have in front of me Mr Eric Messidor and Mr Charlie Laval."

"But what are they doing together at the police

station?"

"That's what you're going to explain to us. Could you come right away please?"

"Yes, of course, I'm coming now."

The moment Eric was being called by the emergency doctor, Charlie arrived at A&E to get tested for swine flu, proof that he was still holding onto his life. He had spotted Eric and had pounced on him. The nurses around had struggled to contain the two men and the ambulance drivers had had to step in to separate them as they were brawling loudly.

The police were called. The two men had been seen by a doctor separately and then taken to the police station handcuffed. That's when my name had come up in both their statements.

When I got to the police station and saw both of their bruised faces, I told myself they were each as bad as the other. I was not allowed to speak to them and was asked to sit in between them as if to make sure they would not jump down each other's throat.

"So now Madam, you're going to tell us your version of the facts. And if I hear any of you two chip in, you're going straight to solitary."

Having to tell the doctor at the airport what had happened on the plane hadn't been easy, but now having to tell everything to the officers about how I had met Charlie, then Eric and why these two had come to fight, was yet another embarrassing moment.

Charlie went pale hearing the story of the plane and Eric too when he heard about my story with Charlie. I tried not to hurt anyone's feelings by keeping Charlie's snoring & jealousy episodes quiet as well as the existence of Eric's wife and children. When I finished my story, the officer said:

"So it's just another sex antics and jealous guys' story…"

Eric, Charlie and I looked at each other sheepishly.

"Ok, it can only be one of two things. Mr Laval, you have assaulted Mr Messidor twice. Either he can decide to file a formal complaint against you or he can decide to leave it here. If it's the latter, I think Mr Messidor would deserve an apology from you Mr Laval. Mr Messidor, if you decide to drop the charges but Mr Laval attacks you again, your three statements are consigned here and they may be used as a witness record in court. It's late and I think everyone wants to go home. Mr Messidor, the choice is yours."

Eric looked at Charlie and said:

"I'll leave it at that."

"Thank you. I'm so sorry. I don't know what's got over me."

"Apologies accepted. But I don't want to see you ever again around Julia."

"Oh no, you can't ask me that."

I spoke:

"That's out of the question. I don't ever want to see you again after what happened."

"Julia, please I'm begging you," cried Charlie.

"No, you've caused enough trouble today. Your behaviour is intolerable. You can delete me from your life now and forever."

I stood up not leaving him any time to answer or we

would be there for another few hours knowing him. Now that I came to think about it, Charlie was a curse of his own!

"Come on Eric, let's go."

Eric didn't need to be asked twice. With that, we left and Charlie broke down in tears, still sitting on his chair. I heard the police officer trying to console Charlie.

"It's going to be alright Mr Laval, it's going to be alright."

I turned around for the last time to see the officer give Charlie a handkerchief. He was a sorry sight.

Eric didn't have anything serious, but his nose had bled quite a lot and he had bruises here and there. I had to play the part of the nurse, which Eric quite enjoyed…

The two weeks that followed were simply delightful. We kept our phones switched off except for one hour during the day. I, to talk to Luana, my mother and listen to Charlie's desperate messages, who was convinced he had the flu and thought it gave him the right to call me. Eric, to talk with his children. He wasn't talking to his wife. We didn't want to watch any TV. It was preferable to keep the media's swine flu hysteria at bay. We only went out to take a walk or buy some food.

Restaurants were empty. People were afraid to get out. When we didn't eat, we made love or slept–especially on the first days when we had a lot of sleep to catch up on– and we talked about our lives. Eric didn't stop telling me how making love to me was like a rebirth.

For fourteen years he had not touched anyone else but his wife. He also told me that he would not be able to lie about what we had been living. They had always told each other everything. Eric didn't think his couple would overcome this. But he couldn't carry on living with his wife as if they were roommates. He didn't want to be separated from his children though and they were the only reason why he could imagine staying with her.

I thought that by the end of the two weeks we might have fallen in love with each other. But it was as if we had become two very good friends who happen to have sex. Friends with benefits as the saying goes... Maybe it was a way to protect ourselves because we knew there was no possible future between us. He had a lot of tenderness for me and I gave it back too.

Our last night before he went back to Bordeaux was a sleepless one. I knew I would never see Eric again. We were determined never to communicate after he left and to consider these past two weeks as a special, unique break in the life of two humans. The last time we made love, was as feverish as it was tender. We were like two lovers trying to remember every inch of each other's skin before we parted. It felt like crying. Because it was the last time I held him against me.

Our story was totally unlikely. Yet it had happened. I can still see Eric's silhouette as he walked away in the street. He had turned around to wave goodbye. I knew this was the last time our eyes would meet.

This curse had forever changed who I was. As well as my perception of morality, my self-confidence and my understanding of the human kind...

CHAPTER 7
STAR FOR A DAY

Eric had left and I was alone in my flat. I hadn't turned on the TV since Mexico. I didn't want to hear any of the media's misleading reports. After all, they were the ones who got the public opinion into this state of total paranoia and who had condemned all the passengers on the plane as if we were all plague stricken.

Now that I was alone, I was curious to see what was being said on the subject. I turned on the TV and was astonished to see my neighbour on the plane being interviewed by a well-known anchorwoman in an afternoon talk-show. The theme of the show was: *How I survived the swine flu*.

She was telling her side of the story: how she had passed the love notes to Eric and took a sleeping pill before she fell asleep. The anchorwoman laughed and said it was the best sex story she had ever heard. I wished the sofa would swallow me up...

Luana called me at that precise moment:

— Turn on the TV!

— I'm in front of it.

— She's alive!

— Yes and if Eric's wife is watching, it's the end! She'd better not pronounce my name.

My neighbour carried on telling how she had felt ill and Luana and I had overcome our fear of the flu and called for help, when no other passenger had lifted a finger. She had learnt it from the medical crew when she woke up because she was unconscious when it had happened. And now she wanted to thank us, but she didn't know our names or how to find us.

I prayed that the passenger list had not been handed over to the TV production and that there was no crew waiting outside my door. The anchorwoman was inviting the viewers to the number on the screen if they had any information.

— Luana, if you call them, you're not longer my friend...

— You don't want people to know about your little adventure on the plane which turned you into a hero? Really Julia, I don't understand you... What about the fifteen minutes of fame in everyone's life? Well that's not all, but how about going on a weekend together now that there is no longer any risk of a curse? We just have to go back to my aunt's house. She just called me to tell me to come next weekend.

— I'm not sure I want to go back to the house where your cousin put a spell on me.

— We can go elsewhere too if you want.

— Jean called me earlier. He wanted us to go to Le Tréport in his house in Normandy. Do you want me to ask him if you can come?

— Isn't he afraid to welcome plague victims?

Apparently not. At the corner bar where we had an aperitif arriving on Friday evening, a guy from Le Tréport had flirted with me, which I had taken as a good sign and just to be sure that the curse was indeed over, I kissed him and closed my eyes lest something else happened. But nothing.

No sudden pain, impromptu vomiting or animal bites of any kind. I was listening anyway in case lightning, a tsunami or a fire destroyed the bar. But no, everything was for the best in the world. My flirting that evening must never have understood why we immediately broke camp, leaving it in the air when the evening seemed to be promising... I didn't need a holiday romance anymore. Now I could finally settle for finding the man of my dreams.

The media continued reporting on the swine flu for about four months. It was contained and never became the world epidemic initially feared. Even if there had been some lethal cases, the disease disappeared progressively from the headlines and other more sensational news took its place...

TABLE OF CONTENTS

THE CURSE OF HOLIDAY ROMANCE

1. THE CURSE..9
2. HOLIDAY IN MEXIO...11
3. ON THE MEXICO-PARIS PLANE................................23
4. EXPLOSIVE NEWS...57
5. THE DAY AFTER...101
6. PARIS..109
7. STAR FOR A DAY..123

A HUGE THANK YOU

Special thanks to Federica for your advice, careful proofreading and for the book layout as well as your support. Thanks to Valerio, Domenico, Jérémie, Lætitia, Laurence and Elisa for your time and patience when proofreading my book in Italian or French and for your precious feedback. Thanks to Judith and Thomas for your eternal support and proof-reading in English.

Thanks to the man, whose inspiration was totally on the mark for the cover: Félix Rousseau.

Thanks to you, my reader who has finished this book! I hope you had a good time with it. If you liked it, recommend it to your friends or leave me a little shout-out on Facebook:

http://www.facebook.com/julialaserie

© June Caravel 2021
Printed by BOD
November 2021